AROMA WITH A VIEW

A NORA BLACK MIDLIFE PSYCHIC MYSTERY
BOOK FOUR

RENEE GEORGE

BARKSIDE OF THE MOON PRESS

Print: February 2021

ISBN: 978-1-947177-38-3

Publisher: Barkside of the Moon Press

"I smell a winner with Renee George's new book, Sense & Scent Ability! The heroine proves that being over fifty doesn't have to stink, even if her psychic visions do."

"Sense & Scent Ability is everything! Nora Black is sassy, smart, and her smell-o-vision is scent-sational. I can't wait for the next Nora book!

For My Father-In-Law, Richard.

His almost 20 years of sobriety from 1986 until he passed away in 2005 was a true inspiration.

He was my pinochle buddy, my friend, and even after sixteen years, I still miss him.

ACKNOWLEDGMENTS

A huge thank you to my "you saved my butt once again" crew of BFFs Robbin, Michele, and Robyn for tirelessly having my back. This story is awesome become of you! Thank you for being my people! I love you guys!

To my editor Kelli Collins. You are a great friend and my rock! I'm sorry I am such a crap client. LOL (The woman is a saint, people!)

To the PWF #13 - Thanks for bringing attention to heroines of a certain age. You ladies are magnificent.

My husband Steve and my son Taylor for taking up the slack around the house, and most of all, leaving me alone to write! I literally couldn't do this without you.

My BFF Dakota Cassidy for being my one true heart when it comes to all things binge-worthy. I love you, girl!

And finally, to the readers. You are making this midlife writer happier than you can even imagine! Thank you for loving Nora and going on this journey with her and her BFF brigade.

My name is Nora Black. I'm over fifty and loving it. I've embraced the aches and pains, hot flashes, and the new odiferous psychic gift that keeps on giving.

My latest smell-o-vision adventure includes a deadly snake, a high-drama baby shower, sibling secrets, and —*surprise*—a murder.

With my two BFFs, my sweetie cop, and a whole bunch of nutty Garden Covians by my side, we'll sniff out the killer. But if we're not careful, we'll come out smelling like...manure.

Forget roses, honey. This aroma with a view is starting to stink.

CHAPTER 1

"And I said, just because you drop a pretty penny for a meal doesn't mean I'm dropping my pretty panties," said Tippi Davenport. She tossed her long blonde hair behind her shoulder and hooted. "And oh, baby, was he ever livid!"

In the living room, a nervous titter of laughter erupted from our guests. Marjorie Meadows, an old friend of my mother's and the Field and Meadows' Art Gallery's co-owner, clapped her hands. "Hah! You said, baby! I get your pin," she said.

The shower guests were playing the diaper pin game. You claimed a safety pin from anyone who spoke the word baby during the shower. The person with the most pins at the end of the party would win a gift certificate to my store, Scents & Scentsability.

I watched Tippi hand over her diaper pin as I readied the next baby shower game of Pass the Pacifier in the dining room area. It appeared the girl could care less about the game because she immediately launched into another ribald tale. *Hoo, boy.*

Gilly Martin walked over to me, holding a glass of orange sherbet, lemon-lime soda, and tropical fruit punch. My BFF since childhood wore a buttery-yellow cashmere sweater that looked lovely against her warm skin tones and dark hair.

"We need to make more of this liquid gold, Nora. That's the last cup." She sniffed the drink. "You'd think this stuff was spiked with premium rum the way these ladies are going through it."

"Nobody sins on a Sunday," I said. We'd picked a Sunday for Pippa's shower because that's when most of the guests were available to attend. "Besides," I added. "Are you sure it isn't spiked?" I gestured toward our loudest guest. "I cannot believe that's Pippa's younger sister." Although the sisters shared a similar fine-boned, willowy appearance, they were definitely polar opposites in the personality department.

Gilly, eyes wide, nodded her agreement. "They say an apple doesn't fall far from the tree, but I'm pretty sure Tippi and Pippa aren't from the same branch."

I gave a low whistle. "I don't think they're from the same tree. If our Pippa is an apple, Tippi is a nut."

Gilly giggled. "Reese looks like she's trying to come up with a good reason to arrest the nut."

Reese McKay was a newly promoted detective with the Garden Cove Police Department, but I'd met her when she was a uniformed patrol officer. I'd helped the local PD with a few cases, and she and I had become friends as a result.

I shrugged. "How much worse could it get?"

Tippi guffawed as she tossed her long blonde hair back, then said, "Whatever you do, don't fall for a married man. I don't care how ugly, emotionally distant, or frigid he says his wife is, he is never going to leave her." Tippi turned her bright blue gaze to Leila Rafferty, my ex-husband's wife, put the back of her hand to her mouth, as if she was going to tell a secret, and added, "I learned that the hard way." She glanced around at her audience and held up two fingers. "Twice."

Leila, who was officially in remission from her cancer after a successful bone marrow transplant last summer, laughed so hard I couldn't help but smile. Leila's cancer had almost killed her, and even though she was still as thin as a rail, she'd put on a couple of pounds in the last few months. I'd lost my mom to cancer almost two years ago in April. When I found out last year that Leila had lost most of her hair to chemo, I'd given her all of my mom's lace front wigs. Today Leila wore a blonde bob number that my mother had loved, and it made me feel like a piece of Mom was still here with me.

Gilly, who could always read my emotions like a book, nudged me gently. "I miss her, too," she said quietly.

I put my head on Gilly's shoulder for the briefest of moments, then used a baby shower napkin to dab my misting eyes.

"I think Dolly is going to implode from embarrassment," whispered Gilly.

I cut my gaze to Dolly Paris, the owner of Dolly's Dollhouse Emporium and Museum, and watched her clutch her pearls. Literally. She wore a strand of cultured pearls and earrings to match. Her gaze darted between her twenty-something daughter Carrie—who seemed enamored with Tippi's stories—and the door.

Jane Beets of Beet's Treats, a candy and sweets shop where I bought brownies way too often, snickered.

Tippi's scandalous behavior proved to be more entertaining for everyone than celebrating my BFF's pregnancy and upcoming wedding. Pippa was miserable, as evidenced by her taking yet another super long bathroom break.

When Pippa rejoined the party, she came up behind me and leaned in. Her voice was tight as she spoke through gritted teeth. "Gilly, why did you invite my sister?"

Gilly flushed. "I thought it would be nice for you to have some family at your baby shower."

"And is it?" Pippa asked. "Is it nice?"

I choked back a laugh. Gilly had extended the invitation to Pippa's mother. But the woman—who had a problem with her daughter having a relationship with *a man of Jordy's ilk*—had summarily declined. I think she might have forgiven Pippa for the pregnancy, but she couldn't forgive her for getting engaged to Jordy. So much so, she cut Pippa off from her allowance.

Of course, up until all this happened, I'd had no idea

Pippa had an allowance. It turns out, her parents own a chain of hotels in Illinois. I mean, I knew Pippa was educated and had excellent taste, but she'd always lived rather modestly. Not like someone who had a lot of cash to burn.

"We're running out of punch," I said. "I'll get some lemon-lime soda from the garage to make more."

"I'll help you," Gilly said.

Pippa grabbed us both. "Oh, no, you don't. You guys will not leave me alone in here with her. Nora, you go distract Tippi while I get the soda."

"I'm not up for another one of Tippi's smell-o-vision memories." Last January, I'd died for twenty-seven seconds on an operating table. After I was revived, I'd developed a talent for seeing scent-related memories. Just not my own memories. The sweet citrus scent of the punch had invoked Tippi's memories of a cheerleading camp where she'd gotten caught playing seven minutes in heaven with a friend's boyfriend. She'd been wearing orange sherbet lip gloss at the time. In the memory, she had been mortified when the closet door had swung open, but today she'd been smiling when she thought of it. "I think your sister has a thing for guys who are unavailable."

"Better lock up your men," Gilly muttered.

Pippa rested her forearms over her basketball-sized belly. "I'm not worried about Jordy."

"The only thing I'm worried about is getting through this next game." A tap at the back door window drew my attention. The face peering back at me through the pane glass made my heart flutter. "Speaking of fellas," I told my besties. "I'll be right back."

I put on my teal puffy winter coat before stepping out into the backyard. Ezra Holden, aka my fella, met me on the deck. He wore gray dress pants, a pale blue button-down shirt, and the same black blazer he'd had on the first time we'd met eleven months ago. It had been an official encounter since he'd been serving me with a restraining order. It felt like ancient history now as Ezra wrapped his arms around me and gave me a kiss.

"Hey, sweetheart."

I melted. "Hey."

He grinned, his eyes crinkling at the corners. "How's the shower going?"

"So far, so good." I chuckled. "You looking for an easy arrest? Because I think Pippa wants to press charges against her sister for...existing."

"Existing is a hard charge to make stick." Ezra slid his hand down my backside and gave my rear a squeeze. "But I might be persuaded to do a twenty-four-hour hold."

I raised up onto my tiptoes and kissed him until a soft moan escaped his lips. Thanks to Lasik surgery in September, I had the eyes of a teenager now, but the best part was being able to see Ezra's gorgeous green eyes clearly when we were this close.

I smiled. "I can be very persuasive."

"You certainly can be," Ezra agreed.

I heard laughter from inside the house, reminding me of my hosting responsibility. "I love this surprise visit.

But I know you wouldn't have come all the way out here just for a stolen kiss."

"You'd be surprised at the lengths I'd go to get a kiss from you."

I let out a giggle that ended on a nervous snort. "All right, then," I said softly. "You better get going now so I can finish up here. You're still coming by tonight, right?"

"Wild horses couldn't keep me away."

Gosh, this man made me giddy. I took a breath to clear my head. "It's a date."

"Perfect." He reluctantly let me go. "Hey, can you tell Reese I'm here? I need to talk to her for a minute."

I raised a brow. "You could've called her."

"Then I wouldn't have gotten to see you in the middle of a workday." He chuckled. "I texted her."

I narrowed my gaze. "She told you to rescue her, didn't she?"

Laughter sparkled in his eyes. "I'm actually here to rescue whoever Tippi is. Reese mentioned the words handcuffs and duct tape in her text."

I gave his chest a quick pat. "Pippa's sister is...er, a lot."

"Sister, huh? I always thought Pippa was an only child."

"She wishes."

He chuckled. "Tell Reese to meet me out front," Ezra said, his tone more serious.

"Hey, is something really wrong?"

He straightened his jacket. "Remember I told you

7

there was a robbery at Meier's Jewelry last week? Reese was the detective on the scene."

"The smash and grab?" Everyone in Garden Cove had heard about the heist. The perpetrators had broken in at the end of the day, forced the owners to disarm the security system, and shattered all the glass displays. The jewelry had been swept clean, and the burglars had managed to escape without leaving any evidence behind. The thieves wore masks and bulky trench coats, so the in-store cameras had been mostly useless in identifying the duo. Shawn Rafferty, my ex and the chief of police, had petitioned the town council for more money to install security cameras downtown, but, so far, the measure hadn't been approved.

I met Ezra's gaze. "Did someone else get robbed?"

"Today," he said. "The Diamond Daisy."

I tucked my chin. "That's Dan Brigg's place. How awful for him. He told me he's barely making ends meet this winter." Many of the businesses in town were hit hard during the off-season. No tourists meant little to no money coming in. Several of the stores in the downtown area, what the locals called the strip, had been closed since November and weren't planning to reopen again until the end of March. Mr. Lems, the man who owned the antique furniture shop next to Scents & Scentsability, had said it was cheaper to close temporarily than to pay to keep the lights on.

Pippa, Gilly, and I had managed to keep our store in the black because of bulk sales of my skin and face lines to a chain of medical spas across the country owned by the celebrity duo of Doctor Corrine and Nurse Mary. Even so, hardly any of these businesses in town, other than a few restaurants and convenience stores, were open on Sundays right now.

"Why was Dan at work today? The Diamond Daisy wasn't opened, was it?" I asked.

Ezra shook his head and frowned. "Mr. Briggs had gone into work to restock shelves and do some maintenance. He said he went into the back of the shop to get some cleaning supplies. And found the burglars waiting for him."

"Is he okay?" Dan was a big man at six and a half feet tall. And he sported a beard that would make the ZZ Top guys jealous. Even in his sixties, he was formidable. "His size alone had to give the thieves pause."

"He said they had guns."

I rubbed my arms. "Cripes. Who robs a souvenir shop?"

"People who don't know it's a souvenir shop," said Ezra. "Locals are aware The Diamond Daisy has nothing to do with diamonds."

The back door opened, and Gilly stuck her head out. "Hey," she hissed. "It's getting tense in here. Tippi is talking about nude yoga, and I think Dolly is one downward-facing-dog story away from an aneurysm."

"I'll be right there," I said. I stared up at Ezra. "I'll send Reese out."

"Love you," he said.

"Love you back."

After Ezra walked away, Gilly dragged me inside the

house. "Pippa is ready to fake contractions to end this baby shower."

"We might have to stuff Tippi into a closet," I said. I went into the living room and put my hand on Reese's shoulder. "Ezra's out front. He says he needs to speak to you."

Reese cast me a grateful and relieved look as she stood up. "Duty calls. Nice party, Nora. Thanks for inviting me." She grabbed her purse, put on her coat, and hurried out the front door like she was escaping prison.

Gilly waved at me from the kitchen. I went to her.

"You cannot leave me alone again." She glanced around conspiratorially. "Pippa can't kill her sister, not yet anyway. But I'm an easier target."

"It's not that bad," I assured her.

She gave me a doubtful look.

I grimaced as our very pregnant and unhappy bestie stalked our way. "Okay. It might be that bad," I admitted. "Maybe I should hide the cake knife."

"Eep," Gilly chirped. "She'll forgive me, though, right?"

"Eventually."

Pippa balled her fists and planted them on her hips. "She's telling them about the time we snuck into the prince's room."

"Which prince? Harry or William?" asked Gilly. "Wait. Why were you at Windsor Castle?"

"I wasn't. I'm talking about Prince Carl Phillip of Sweden," she said. "At the penthouse suite at my parent's hotel in Chicago."

"I've never heard of him, but wowza," Gilly said, awe-struck. "Your parents know royalty?"

"Not really. The king had some business in the city, and my parents had a penthouse suite available." She smirked. "However, Prince Carl Phillip is gorgeous. He could give that guy from the *Fifty Shades* movies a run for his money."

I raised a brow at Gilly. "That's a story I want to hear later."

"Maybe when this baby is out, and I can tell it over a glass of wine." Pippa smiled at Gilly. Her sister laughed loudly again, and Pippa's smile turned to a sneer. She lightly punched my shoulder. "Fix this, or I'll swap out labels on your soap-making supplies."

I gasped with mock outrage. "You wouldn't dare." I could see my friend was in distress, and, considering she was eight months pregnant, I didn't want to make her more miserable. Not even with a well-intentioned cele-bration. "Maybe we should just skip right to the cake and presents and get the party over with."

"Can we?" asked Pippa with such hope in her voice, I felt my stomach drop. I hadn't realized how close to the emotional edge Pippa felt.

Before I could answer, Carrie shouted, "Mom!"

The three of us moved quickly into the living room. Dolly sat on the couch gasping noisily as she rummaged through her purse.

"Is she having a panic attack?" Tippi asked. "I've had one of those before. So not fun."

Gilly moved into rescue mode and made a beeline for

the woman. Dolly, whose name conjured up visions of Dolly Parton, was the exact opposite of the iconic singer. She was a few years older than me, but her gray hair was styled in what Gilly liked to call "nursing home chic." She also dressed like a retired librarian.

Gilly undid the top pearl button of Dolly's pink cardigan. "Are you okay, sweetheart?"

Carrie frantically dug through her mom's purse. "It's not in here," the younger Paris said.

"What are you looking for? An EpiPen?" I asked. The way Dolly was struggling to breathe made me think it was something more serious than a panic attack. "Is she having an allergic reaction?" Had the white chocolate chunk cookies I'd served for the party caused some kind of anaphylaxis reaction? I grasped Carrie's wrist to get her attention. "Does your mom have a nut allergy?"

Carrie, a dark-haired girl in her late twenties, shook her head. "I'm looking for her inhaler. She doesn't have food allergies. She has stress-induced asthma."

Pippa cast an accusing glance at her sister. Tippi bugged her eyes. "I only mentioned one Kama Sutra position. We hadn't even gotten to the Lotus position yet."

"Oh, dear God," muttered Pippa. She glared at her sister. "Stop. Talking."

Tippi pressed her lips together and scooted back into her chair.

"Do you remember putting the inhaler in your purse before we left?" Carrie asked her mom.

Dolly nodded, then rasped through sips of breaths, "Yes."

Carrie frowned. "She keeps a back-up in her car. I'll get it." The young woman jogged to the door, flung it open, and exited the house, leaving the front door wide open.

I stifled a groan. It wasn't freezing out, but it was below fifty degrees, and not only was the heat escaping, but my electric bill was going up.

Gilly leaned Dolly forward and grabbed the nearest coffee cup. She paused, leaned in for a long sniff, and wrinkled her nose. "This has alcohol in it."

"Damn it, Tippi," Pippa said.

Tippi brought her hands up. "It's not mine."

Pippa scoffed. "Yeah, right."

Gilly wasn't having any of the sisters' arguments. "Enough. We need a stimulant, not a depressant," she said. "Someone grab me a cup of black coffee. Hold the vodka."

"Oh, for Pete's sake," Pippa said with exasperation.

Tippi hopped up from the couch. "I'll get it." She headed to the kitchen.

"How do you know all this stuff about asthma?" Marjorie asked Gilly.

"My daughter Ari had a friend in fifth grade who was asthmatic. I learned a lot about how to help ease breathing during an attack with what you have on hand. Coffee is a stimulant, so it dilates the lungs. If worse comes to worst, we can put her in the bathroom and steam up the room by turning on hot water taps."

I nodded. "If worse comes to worst, I'm dialing 9-1-1."

"Already on it," Pippa said as she pulled her phone from her purse.

Dolly tried to stand. "No," she said. "Don't...call. I'll..be oh..okay."

A scream from outside brought all the chaos in the room to an abrupt stop.

"Carrie," Dolly wheezed. "That's Carrie."

CHAPTER 2

*E*zra stood near the open driver door of Dolly's gold hatchback, which was parked at the end of my driveway facing the house. He held one hand out toward the car and had one hand on his gun. Carrie sat in the driver's seat, but it was hard to see her with the sun glinting off the windshield.

Reese was on the passenger side of the car, her phone to her ear. Her face was pale, but her expression was determined.

I jogged toward them. "What happened?"

"Stay back, Nora," Ezra demanded. His fierce tone stopped me in my tracks. "Carrie, I need you to keep holding as still as possible. Don't make any sudden moves."

Had Carrie done something illegal?

"Carrie." Dolly stumbled across the lawn, apparently recovered from her asthma attack. "What's going on? Why are you holding my daughter hostage?"

"Ma'am, you need to stay back," Ezra cautioned.

A high-pitched squeal escaped the young woman.

"Carrie!" her mother shouted. Gilly slung her arm around Dolly's shoulders, comforting her but also keeping the panicked mother from rushing toward the car. All the guests from the party now stood on my lawn, their gazes locked on the car.

I walked slowly around toward the passenger side. Reese, who was standing in front of the open door, shook her head at me.

"What's this about?" I mouthed.

She held up a finger. "Yes, hello," she said into the phone. "This is Detective Reese McKay. I need animal control and an ambulance dispatched to Hawthorne Subdivision, 602 Dogwood Court. "

"Animal control?" I decided Ezra wasn't angry. He was scared. But of what? I tried to cycle through all the animals that might be out in the winter. Raccoons, maybe. Cougar? Doubtful. Maybe a rabid squirrel? Probably not. I was reasonably sure opossums held up in dens during the winter. I slow-walked to the grass, joining the baby shower guests.

Pippa sidled next to me. "Do you know what's going on?"

"Ezra," I said with a measured tone. "Give us the quick and dirty. You have a yard full of freaked-out witnesses, and one of them is Carrie's mom."

"Snake," Ezra said. "A great big copperhead, I think. It's in the floorboard, so it's hard to tell for sure."

Dolly gasped, her breathing turning into a harsh wheeze once again. "Oh..." she gulped. "Oh, no."

I glanced at Gilly.

She nodded. "I've got her."

"Please help me," Carrie whimpered.

"Help is on the way. Hold real still now," Ezra cautioned again. "A sudden move could make it strike."

"Are you kidding me with this?" Tippi said in a hushed whisper from behind Pippa and me. "I thought living in a small town would be boring, but this is the most excitement I've had in months."

"I find that hard to believe," Pippa said.

Tippi crossed her arms and frowned but said nothing else.

I took Pippa's fine-boned hand and gave it a squeeze. "You don't see any snakes this time of year," I said. "Let alone poisonous ones."

Reese, who was off the phone now, nodded. "Yes. They usually hunker down in a rock den until spring."

"It's moving," Carrie said. "I feel it wrapping around my foot."

"Does anyone have a flashlight?" It was forty-seven degrees outside, but Ezra's face was flushed, his forehead beaded with sweat. "I want to get a better look at it."

"I've got one," Leila said. She pulled a yellow mini flashlight from her purse and trotted over to Ezra. "And don't worry," she directed at Carrie. "Snakes don't like the cold, probably why it's in the front floorboard. It's trying to soak up some engine warmth. The light from a flashlight doesn't generate any heat." She handed the mini to Ezra.

"Thank you, Mrs. Rafferty." He clicked the flashlight on and shone the beam toward Carrie's feet and swore. "Cripes." Ezra's mouth was set in a grim line. "It's got to be at least five feet long, and it's coiled around the foot pedals."

"See," Leila said, craning her neck around the door for a better look. "It's just trying to stay warm." She gave a low whistle. "Wow. That sucker looks well-fed, too. You should call Johnny Scales."

"Who?" Ezra asked. I wasn't familiar with the name either, but Reese was.

"Johnny 'Scales' Morrison has a snake farm about fifteen miles outside of town. Still in the county, but rural," she said. "He's pure weirdo."

Leila circled around Ezra. "Johnny's something of a character, but he's great with snakes. Shawn hired him two years ago when we found a rattler in our garage. Johnny had it out of there in minutes. No muss, no fuss."

Ezra shook his head. "Animal control is on the way. I'm sure they can handle it."

"How did it get in my mom's car?" Carrie asked. I'd moved around for a better view, along with a few of the baby shower guests.

I caught a glint of the snake, and just the sight of shiny scales made my teeth hurt.

"Copperheads are really poisonous, right?" Pippa asked.

"They really are." I rubbed my arms to ward off the

willies. I heard the sirens in the distance before I saw the ambulance coming up the street. I hoped like hell we wouldn't need it. "Will they have antivenom?"

Reese answered, "No, but the hospital keeps antivenom for poisonous snakes in our area. If it's a copperhead, they should have it on hand, just in case someone gets bitten."

"Has that happened?"

Reese shrugged. "Not that I know of. At least not since I've been with the GCPD. But it's one of the things we were briefed about during rookie orientation. Fortunately, death by snake bite is a rarity."

The ambulance stopped in the middle of the street. Our guests' vehicles had taken up mine and Gilly's driveways and most of the real estate by our curbs. I recognized the driver as Bob, the same paramedic who had checked me out the first time I'd passed out during an intense vision. His partner was a young blond man, a little taller than Ezra, and with Captain America looks.

The Chris Evans lookalike glanced around. "Where's the patient?"

"Over here," Tippi waved. "I think I need CPR."

The hot paramedic shook his head, a bare hint of a smile on his lips.

"Grant," said Carrie. "I n-need help."

I shared a look with Gilly. Carrie knew the young EMT?

"Oh, my God." Grant headed toward the driver's side, but Reese's stern voice stopped him.

"Stay back," she ordered.

Ezra kept his gaze on the snake, his shoulders bunched with tension. The EMT hit the brakes, his face flushed, but I didn't know if it was from embarrassment or concern for Carrie.

"Over here." Reese didn't even try to conceal her annoyance. "No snake bite yet, but we need you just in case."

He walked to where Reese stood and looked inside the car. "Holy moly." His eyes widened. "Carrie…oh, crap. That's a huge freaking snake."

"It's moving again, Grant!" Carrie yelped. "I have to get out of here. I have to—"

"Stop," said Bob as Grant rounded the front of the car. "Go get supplies ready."

"But—"

"No buts, probie. Go."

Given his mutinous expression, I didn't think Grant would do as Bob said. But after a moment's hesitation, he jogged toward the ambulance.

Bob moved to Ezra's side. "Stay calm, Carrie. The snake is as afraid of you as you are of it."

"I doubt that." Carrie's knuckles were white, her face red, and tears streamed down her cheeks. Her arms began to tremble involuntarily. "I'm not going to make it," she said. "I'm not sure I can hold still."

"Even if you do get bitten, you won't die," Bob assured her as he imparted the same information Reese had just given us. He paused. "You're not allergic to snake venom, are you?"

Carrie looked at Bob like he was crazy. "How would I know that?" she said, her voice rising.

"You're not allergic, honey," called out Dolly. "I had you tested when you were young."

Bob smiled. "Then you're fine."

I glanced at Dolly. I knew she was a protective mother, but why on earth would she get her young child tested for snake poison allergies? That seemed rather extreme.

"The Discovery Channel had a whole series on poisonous snakes. You're supposed to keep your heart rate slow and low," Pippa offered.

Tippi added, "You know, if she were a honey badger, she would not give a f—"

"Hey," Pippa said. "Not. The. Time." I had a feeling she'd said that a lot to her sister over the years.

"Where's animal control?" Ezra asked.

Bob shook his head. "We were dispatched for a probable snake bite. That's all I know."

"Reese," Ezra said.

She already had her phone out. "On it."

"It's moving up my legs," said Carrie, her voice hoarse from crying.

"It must be getting colder in the floorboard," Leila said. "Carrie's body is the best heat source."

"Could something cold drive it away from Carrie?" I asked.

It was a question no one could answer.

"It's on my thiii-igheee!" Carrie squeaked. "Help."

I saw the thick, slithering brown and cream-colored snake clearly now as the sunlight hit its scaly head. My stomach did a backflip and several somersaults. Even from here, I saw Carrie's slight body trembling. I didn't know if she moved suddenly or if her shaking startled the snake, but it opened its mouth wide and struck. Its fangs sunk into her forearm.

Carrie screamed.

Dolly cried out and nearly collapsed, but Gilly had her by the shoulders and managed to prop up the woman. The poor lady couldn't speak, but the silent tears rolling down her cheeks said plenty about her fear for her daughter.

"Animal control is ten minutes out," Reese told us.

All I could think about was Leila saying snakes didn't like the cold. We needed something cold to get the snake away from Carrie. My pulse raced as I ran into the house and grabbed the small fire extinguisher from the kitchen. It was a carbon dioxide fire extinguisher. Last week, I set a pan on fire, which was another reason I didn't cook. But I knew from that experience the spray was very, very cold.

I pulled the pin as I left the house and ran across the yard, ignoring the twinge in my right knee. When I got to the car, Ezra asked, "What are you doing?"

"Trying to save Carrie. Hold your breath and close your eyes," I ordered.

She was pale and barely responsive. I don't know if the poison worked that fast or if she was going into shock. Either way, I blasted the beast of a snake with the CO_2 extinguisher before anyone could protest. The snake recoiled but didn't strike, so I shot it with the spray once more. It slithered toward the passenger side. Reese took several steps away.

"Hit it again," Ezra said.

I laid into it with one long blast, and the snake moved sluggishly out the open door. The cold appeared to slow it down as it slithered out the passenger side. Reese pressed her booted foot down on its neck just below the head. It didn't even squirm that much.

"Got it," she exclaimed.

I let out a quick sigh of relief.

"Great work, Nora." The pride in Ezra's voice warmed me. "That was quick thinking."

Carrie's gaze flicked up to me. "Thank you," she whispered. "Thank..." Her eyes rolled back as she slumped over and passed out.

Bob pushed his way past me, a stack of gauze and a rolled bandage in hand.

"She's unconscious, but she won't be for long." He pushed up the sleeve of her shirt and placed the gauze over the puncture marks. He wrapped the forearm from above the wound to just below it with the bandage, then affixed it with tape he'd removed from his pocket.

"Don't you need to cut the bite marks and suck out the poison?" Tippi asked seriously.

Pippa gave her a stern look.

Tippi frowned. "That's what they do in movies."

"Nope," Bob said. "We don't use tourniquets either. All of that will just make the situation worse. Right now, I need to get Carrie to the emergency department with as little movement on her part as possible." Bob jerked his chin up. "Grant. I need a splint."

The young man handed him a plastic wrist stabilizer, another rolled bandage, and a sling. "I'll get the gurney."

"Awesome," Bob muttered as he applied the brace.

"Can I help?" I asked.

Carrie moaned as she came around. She blinked rapidly then her eyes widened in horror. "Oh my gosh, I feel like I'm burning. Oh, oh." Tears leaked down her cheeks as she shifted her legs.

"Don't move," Bob directed gently. "Even small movements will make the snake venom circulate through your body faster." He unlocked his phone and handed it to me. "Can you take pictures of the snake, please? One of the head and one of the body will be enough."

I took Bob's cell phone to the other side of the car. It took me a second to figure out how to get his camera to come up. Reese held still as I carefully documented the venomous creature pinned under her boot. After, I returned the phone to the paramedic.

Bob slid it into his pocket. He finished immobilizing Carrie's arm, then slid a ring off her right hand and handed it to me—a silver band with turquoise hearts set in it. "Just in case her hands swell," he said.

Carrie's legs began to shake as her face contorted. "I don't know if I can hold still. I feel like my arm is on fire."

Grant brought the gurney onto my lawn. I moved out of the way as he dropped it down and took a syringe that had been resting on the pillow. "Morphine," he said to Bob as he popped the cap.

"Carrie, are you allergic to any medications?" Bob asked.

"No," yelled Dolly as she staggered toward the car. "She's not."

Carrie moaned. "Help me. Please, God, help me."

Bob nodded to Grant, and the young paramedic administered the injection. After, the EMTs made quick work extracting Carrie from the vehicle, getting her on the gurney, and into the ambulance.

Dolly's wheezing increased as she walked to the ambulance. I ran over to the car. "Where do you keep your extra inhaler?" I called out.

Dolly said something I couldn't hear, but Gilly said, "She says it's in her glove box."

My skin felt like it was crawling as I quickly slid into the driver seat, leaned over, and popped the glove box open. I took out some napkins, some motion sickness pills and finally saw the red inhaler. The snake under Reese's foot hissed. A jolt of panic hastened my retreat from the vehicle.

I was still trembling as I handed Dolly her medicine. Dolly shook the small device then sucked in a spray of it before noisily blowing it out. She put her hand on the bay door before Grant could shut it. "I'm going with you."

"Ma'am, we can't let civilians—"

"That's my daughter," she insisted.

"I'm sorry," Grant said.

Gilly put her arm around Dolly. "I'll take you to the hospital," Gilly told her. Then she nodded to the paramedics. "We'll meet you there."

CHAPTER 3

"*L*and sakes, that was the scariest thing I've been through in a long time," Marjorie Meadows said. "I've never heard of a snake coming out in the dead of winter. I mean, I know we've had a few warm days, but this is ridiculous." Marjorie was in her early seventies and still extremely active in the community. The older woman had lost her husband in her forties, and she and my mom had become close friends after they'd met in a widow support group. Even so, she took great care of herself and could probably run circles around most of us.

"It was huge, too." Tippi's eyes were wide. Maybe seeing Carrie taken away on a gurney had sobered her up. "I have a friend with a python, and that snake out there was definitely bigger."

"I've never seen one that big before." Leila nodded. "At least, not in the wild. Granted, it's not like we get a lot of copperheads around Garden Cove."

Ezra had waited with Reese until the animal control unit arrived and retrieved the snake out from under her foot. Reese stayed calm and collected. Even so, ten to fifteen minutes was a long time to wait when you have an angry snake coiling its tail around your ankle. Her relief was obvious as the two men took control of the situation, using snake tongs, a hook, and a bag to retrieve and control the poisonous pest.

After, Ezra had given me Dolly's keys. I put them in a pink Depression candy dish on the oak console near my front door. I remembered I'd pocketed Carrie's ring and dropped it into the dish as well. I'd give them to Dolly when she came for the car.

As I returned to the remaining guests, I thought about Leila's comments about the scarcity of copperheads around Garden Cove. I'd grown up in the area, and she was right. They weren't common. At least not in populated areas.

"It is strange," I said. "I've never seen one up close and personal until today."

"That fire extinguisher was quick thinking on your part," Jane said. "How in the world did you come up with that idea?"

I shook my head with a chuckle. "If I hadn't burnt up a frying pan trying to cook bacon a few days ago, I wouldn't have thought of it. So, I guess we have my poor skills in the kitchen to thank. Well, that and the fact that Gilly bought me a replacement cylinder." I smiled as I thought of my BFF. She took such good care of people— just the way she was taking care of Dolly right now.

"Snakes don't want to be around people about as much as people want to be around snakes," Marjorie said. "My son Davis ran into a rattlesnake perched on a low branch once when he was a teenager. Damn fool was out running in the woods, jumped up and grabbed the branch to do a pull-up, and found himself face to face with the nasty beast. That boy screamed so loud I thought his butt was on fire."

A few of us laughed, but Pippa barely smiled as she moved away from the group and headed toward the kitchen.

I followed her out of the living room and out of earshot to our guests. "You're fading," I told her. "Are you okay?"

"Tired," she admitted. "I know it sounds ungrateful, Nora, but can we get to the gifts and cake?"

"I'm sorry about Tippi. Gilly meant well."

"I know." Pippa sighed. "My relationship with my family is contentious. And that's putting it nicely."

"Will you be okay without the allowance? I can see if there's any money in our budget to give you a raise."

"There isn't," she said quickly. Pippa did the books, so she would know. "Besides, I'll be fine without it. Most of what my parents gave me is in a savings account. And since I've moved in with Jordy, there's no need to keep my apartment."

"Still, I'm sorry."

"It's okay." She put her arm around my shoulders. "Just don't go inviting any of my family to the wedding."

I chuckled and crossed my heart. "Not even if they bribed me."

"You won't need to worry about that." She smiled, but it was tight and didn't reach her eyes. I think her parents' disapproval bothered her more than she wanted to admit.

"I'm sure they want what they consider best for you," I told her. "Even if they are more wrong than they'll ever know. It's probably from a place of love, though."

"Hah," she replied quietly. "They want to control me. They always have. Honestly, after I followed you here to Garden Cove, I thought they would cut me off then. So, I've been preparing myself to live without their support for a while. I don't need them." She paused and then patted her belly. "Though Junior here will benefit from their generosity. He or she already has a nice fat college fund."

"That's my Pippa. You are a strong, kick-ass, independent woman." I slipped my arm around her waist. "But that doesn't mean you can't miss your family or want them in your life."

"I have Jordy. And you and Gilly." She patted her belly. "And soon, this one. So, I have all the family I need."

Tippi poked her head around the corner. "You okay, Pip? Can I help with anything?"

"You can give me a little peace and quiet," Pippa snapped.

Tippi winced. She gave Pippa a thumbs up and kept her tone upbeat. "You got it."

Pippa grimaced as Tippi returned to the living room.

"I should apologize, but I can't help but wonder why she's even here." Her tone was suspicious.

"Your sister might be a lot," I told Pippa. "But she showed up. That's something, right?"

"It's something," Pippa allowed. She shook her head. "I don't like to think about my past, especially where my family is concerned. But…well, keep an eye on anything of value in the house." Her expression grew pained. "Tippi has stolen from me countless times. Once, she visited me in college and took my roommate's heirloom necklace. She was seventeen when that happened, and it got worse from there." The memory darkened her light blue eyes. "Tippi had a credit card our parents gave her, so it wasn't as if she needed money. After I found my roommate's necklace in her purse, she didn't even apologize. Just laughed it off."

"Wow, that's awful."

Pippa sighed. "Tippi's always been impulsive and self-ish. She can't be shamed, either. And she can't be trusted, Nora."

"All right. I'll keep an eye on her." I cast a glance up the hallway. "But right now, why don't I get this party shut down?"

"Thank you." Her relief made me sad. She'd been looking forward to the baby shower when we'd been in the planning stages. Thanks to her sister, she wasn't enjoying it at all. "I need to get home and off my feet."

I glanced down at her swollen ankles. "Go lay down in the guest bedroom," I said, ushering her down the hall toward my spare room. "I'll clear the place out."

She gave me a wan smile. "Tell them to leave the gifts."

I smiled back. "I'll frisk them at the door."

"See? This is why you're my BFF," she said. Then she grasped her belly and *oofed*.

"Everything okay?"

"I think Baby Davenport-Hines is going to be a boxer."

I smirked. "She'll be a prizefighter."

"Or he," Pippa said. She narrowed her gaze at me. "You didn't break into my doctor's office, did you?"

"Your child's gender is safely a secret. Though why you'd want to be surprised in this day and age is beyond me."

"Don't mention age," Pippa groaned. "If I have to hear about how dangerous a *geriatric* pregnancy is one more time, I'm going to snatch my doctor by her short and curlies."

"It's definitely an antiquated phrase. I mean, you're barely thirty-seven. It's not as if your uterus is a dried-up dusty husk."

"Descriptive," she said dryly.

"I just mean, there's still life in those reproductive organs."

Pippa snorted. "Literally." Her smile slipped away as she wistfully touched her belly. "It's not just Tippi being here that's got me frazzled, you know. The whole Carrie getting snake bit at my baby shower feels like a bad omen."

"What are you worried about, Pip? You've had all the tests. You and that baby have passed with flying colors. If a pregnancy was a university, you'd be on track for summa cum laude. In a month or so, you will deliver us a happy, healthy boy or girl. And, frankly, I can't wait to start spoiling the little sweetheart."

"Logically, I know you're right. Jordy keeps telling me the same, but the closer I get to my due date, the more I worry."

"I think a cyclops with three legs would've shown up on an ultrasound."

"Not funny." She smacked my arm. "You're going to give me nightmares."

"Baby Davenport-Hines is going to be gorgeous, just like his or her mom and dad. Now, go rest while I corral the guests."

Pippa went into the guest room, and I closed the door between us.

When I walked into the living room, all eyes pivoted toward me. Before I opened my mouth, Leila jumped up from the couch and grabbed two coffee cups and an empty serving tray from the coffee table. "Why don't we help Nora get this place cleaned up and be on our way?"

Without Gilly here as backup, it was nice to have Leila step up. I cast her a grateful look. "I'm afraid our mom-to-be has had all the excitement she can stand for one day."

Tippi got up. Her demeanor was more subdued than I'd seen it all afternoon. "Point me in the right direction."

I led her to the kitchen, grabbed a trash bag from under the sink, and handed it to her. "If you could gather up all the napkins, plates, cups, and such. That would be a big help."

Leila dumped a coffee cup into the sink. I instantly smelled the booze as hot water from the faucet hit the dregs.

Tippi's face pinched as she reached out for the trash bag.

"I can't do this with you anymore. It stopped being cute a long time ago," a man says. His hair is light brown. He is tall and broad-shouldered. I can't see his face because I never see faces in my visions, but his voice is low and grim.

"I'll quit, Jack," the woman says. She has lighter hair, and she and the man are of similar height. "Just give me time."

"I've given you five months."

The woman's tone turns from pleading to menacing. "Who knew getting sober would turn you into such a bitch."

"I love you, Tip," he says with calm deliberateness as he walks away. "I probably always will. But I'm done."

Tippi took the bag from me. "On it," she said as she walked out of the kitchen.

Marjorie came over to me. The crease between her eyes deepened as she frowned. "Are you okay? Maybe you should go sit down."

I forced a smile and shook my head. "I'm fine." After my involvement with two different murder cases in Garden Cove, rumors about my psychic ability had made the rounds. Fortunately, most people dismissed the stories as bunk. I hoped Marjorie was one of them. "I'm worried about Carrie, is all." I glanced at my phone sitting on the counter. "Gilly should have called by now."

As if conjured, my cell phone lit up with Gilly's name.

Marjorie smiled. "Ask, and ye shall receive."

"It's nice when it works out that way." Most of the baby shower guests had come into the kitchen when my phone rang, so I put Gilly on speaker. "How's Carrie?" I asked.

"She's gotten the antivenom, and the doctor is admitting her for observation."

"Dolly must be out of her head," Leila said.

"After the initial shock wore off, she calmed down. The doctor said this is the first snake bite the hospital has seen in eight years. He was stunned that it happened in February."

I was astonished as well. I'd seen firsthand how much the snake had hated the cold. Why would it have left its den to slither up into Dolly's car? "It's nuts," I agreed. "I'm glad Carrie got to the hospital in time."

"According to the doctor, copperhead bites aren't usually fatal, just painful as heck. He said it would take a couple of weeks to fully recover, though. She can expect a lot of swelling and pain until she fully heals."

"Then why are they admitting her?" Jane asked. "I mean, if she's not in any danger?"

Gilly answered. "The antivenom can have some nasty side effects. Something called serum sickness, so Scott, err…" she cleared her throat "…the doctor wants her at the hospital to manage symptoms if that happens."

I raised a brow at Leila. She let slip a barely-there smile.

"Scott, huh?"

The mood was palpably lighter now that we knew Carrie was on the mend. The ladies around me snickered.

"Well, that's all I know," Gilly said quickly as if she hadn't heard me. "Oh, and Dolly left her purse in the living room. The hospital needs Carrie's insurance card, and she didn't have it on her. Dolly keeps a spare in her wallet."

I carried the phone into the living room. Dolly's satchel purse was next to the couch. "It's here. Do you want me to bring it to the hospital?"

"No, just find the card and take a picture of it, front and back. Text it to me. They can get started on the claim with that, and Dolly can bring the card here tomorrow for an official scanning."

"What about her car?"

"Dolly's worn out, so I'm going to take her home after they get Carrie settled. Are you good with us dropping her car to her in the morning?"

"Sounds like a plan."

"I'm sorry I'm not there helping you with all the baby shower stuff."

"Don't even worry about it. We're pretty much done here." I cast my cleaning crew a grateful look. "See you soon."

"See you," Gilly replied, then hung up.

I rummaged through Dolly's purse. Boar bristle hairbrush, a lipstick case, sanitizing wipes, a small jar of petroleum jelly, travel tissue, a note pad, a compact case. I cussed when I poked my finger on the end of a small pair of pointy scissors. I found her inhaler hiding in a side pouch under pens and a couple of Chapsticks. I considered dumping the purse until I finally saw the wallet.

However, my jaw dropped when I saw the shiny object nestled in next to it—an empty travel-sized bottle of vodka.

Two things came to mind. The spiked coffee hadn't been Tippi's, after all. And why was sweet, innocent Dolly day-drinking at a baby shower?

CHAPTER 4

The next morning Gilly knocked on my door. Ezra ended up canceling our plans because of work, but I'd been depleted from the day's events, so it had been a bad news-good news situation for me. Bad, I didn't get to see Ezra. Good, I slept like a rock.

"Morning, Nora. You ready to go?" Her hair was pulled back and cinched with a pretty, jeweled butterfly comb on one side. Several strands around her face and the crown of her head were extremely lighter than her normally dark brown. Her make-up was a little heavier than her normal daytime look, and she wore black jeans with a chocolate brown turtleneck sweater that showed off all her best assets.

"Well, don't you look like the prize cow," I said teasingly. It was something my dad used to say whenever I would get dressed up for school events. "And did you put new highlights in your hair?"

Gilly rolled her eyes. "Ari did it for me last night. We

bought one of those pull-through highlight kits. I styled my hair this way because the color is too patchy. I'm going to try and fix it tonight."

"It looks really nice the way you have it."

Gilly smiled at the compliment. "I told Dolly we'd drop her car off before eight, so let's get a move on."

"I see. You gussied up for Dolly, huh?"

She shrugged and patted her hair. "I thought we could stop by the hospital and check on Carrie."

"And Scott?" I asked.

She feigned astonishment. "Now, Nora, what kind of woman do you think I am?"

"The kind that would get dressed up at seven in the morning to impress a cute doctor."

She frowned then laughed. "You're not wrong."

"Not that I don't approve of you playing the field, but I thought you and Luke were hitting it off." Luke Robson was a security supervisor at a hotel in the city. We'd met him in August when we'd gone to a beauty convention for my birthday. Luke was an army veteran and, most importantly, a nice guy. He and Gilly had met up a few times since that weekend, but they both had complicated lives.

"We are. We do," Gilly said. "But we're having an… adult relationship, you know. Taking it slow."

"How slow?"

"A snail moves faster," she said with a grimace. "I don't know. Luke asked me to move to the city to be with him, but my life is here, Nora. My kids, my house, my job." She gave me a meaningful look. "My friends."

"Your friends are going to be your friends no matter where you go. As to the rest, I get it." My stomach clenched at the idea of Gilly moving away. It dawned on me how awful it must have been for her when I'd first left Garden Cove. She never tried to talk me out of it, though. And I would give her the same support if she ever genuinely wanted to leave. "Is there a part of you that wants to go?"

Her eyes went to that far-off place where possibilities are endless before she met my gaze. "I don't. I would love to be with Luke, truly. He makes me happy…adjacent. I love how I feel when I'm around him, but I don't want to start my life over in a new place. I like what I've built here."

"And if he moved to Garden Cove?"

"I would love it. But I think it would be the same for him. He likes where he's at."

I gave her a hug. "I'm proud of you."

She dropped her chin and smirked. "For what?"

"For knowing your own mind. That's not always easy. And not just for that." I thought about how she'd been with Dolly the day before. Gilly was the best person I knew. "I'm always proud of you, by the way. I'm so happy you're in my life."

"Did someone forget to change their hormone patch?" Gilly teased, but her voice cracked, and her eyes glistened with unshed tears. "If this world was a stormy sea, you'd be my lighthouse, Nora."

"I feel the same way." I let her go. "Get some coffee. I'll be right back, and we can go."

"You did forget to change your patch." She snickered.

I ignored her as I headed down the hall to the bathroom, where I kept my hormone patches.

DOLLY PARIS' home was an A-frame house on the cove about two miles past the Portman's on the Lake Resort entrance. The resort was owned by Claire Portman. Although, since her husband's incarceration for all manner of white-collar crimes, she had relegated the day-to-day running of the business to her son Roger and his wife, Kati. Kati, as it happened, was Ezra's ex-wife and the mother of his teenage son Mason. Eight years ago, he'd followed his ex-wife and son to Garden Cove, leaving behind a promising law enforcement career in the big city. He was a father first and a cop second.

I grabbed Dolly's keys and Carrie's ring from the dish on my console, along with Dolly's cavernous purse to take back to her. I'd never been to Dolly's place before but followed Gilly easily enough. I'd given her the keys and made her drive the snake car, though. The idea of getting into that vehicle after a copperhead had been slithering around in it gave me the heebie-jeebies. Luckily, my BFF was made of sterner stuff.

We parked in Dolly's narrow driveway and got out. The lake was visible, even from the front of the house. "This place has an amazing view," I said.

"It sure does," Gilly agreed. "Dolly bought it for a steal

when she moved back to Garden Cove. Twenty-five or so years ago, there wasn't near as many resorts."

I grabbed Dolly's purse from the car before we headed to the porch. "I never knew Dolly had moved away. "

Gilly nodded. "Right after you left for college, she ran off with some guy from Rasfield. She came home a few years later with a kid in tow and a whole new puritanical way of living."

I searched my recollection, but, really, until recent years, Dolly hadn't been in my orbit of thoughts. She'd been older, and we'd never hung out together. Our recent friendship had developed because we both owned local shops near each other.

"I can't believe I didn't know any of this." Although maybe her complicated past explained the bottle of booze in her purse. I couldn't help but think of the parallels between Dolly's struggles and those of Tippi. I stood by Pippa no matter what. However, my instincts leaned toward Tippi making a genuine attempt to connect with her older sister.

Gilly shrugged. "When she returned, Dolly was pretty far from the wild child of her youth. And the town had moved on to bigger and better scandals."

"As they do," I said.

Gilly smiled. "Let's give her the keys and her purse and get going. Otherwise, we're not going to have time to stop by the hospital before my first client at eight-thirty."

"Drop me off at the shop first," I said as we climbed

the porch steps. "Pippa isn't feeling well, so I want to get in and help her open this morning."

"Yesterday was a disaster," Gilly said. "I had no idea inviting her sister would cause such a stir."

"Your heart was in the right place," I told her. "Pippa knows that." I rang the doorbell and waited. "Besides, I have a feeling Tippi isn't here for anything nefarious. I think she wants to be near Pippa—and maybe even get some forgiveness for past actions."

Gilly gave me a flat look. "I don't know about that." Dolly hadn't answered the doorbell, so Gilly knocked. "That's strange. She knew we were coming by." She twisted the doorknob. It wasn't locked, which wasn't unusual for rural living. Gilly opened the door. "Dolly," she called out. "It's Gilly and Nora. Are you up?"

We heard nothing. "That's weird," I said. "Do you think she got a ride into town from someone else?"

"Maybe. But why not wait until we got here? Surely, she'd prefer to use her own car, and she needs the insurance card for the hospital." Gilly opened the door all the way and stepped inside.

"We shouldn't—"

Gilly's gasp cut my caution short. She rushed inside, and I followed.

Once in, I saw Dolly on the floor, a pool of dark blood crowning her head of graying hair. Gilly squatted next to her and felt for a pulse. She shook her head. "She's gone."

As I stumbled closer, I was struck by the scent of alcohol, some kind of woodsy aroma, and a whiff of rotting garbage.

"Tell me," the voice is menacing, deadly. "Tell me where you hid the money and jewels, or I will destroy everything and everyone you love." He pushes a trembling blonde woman against the wall of a room I don't recognize.

"He's dead," she cries out. "And it's our fault. No guns," she says. "We said, no guns."

He shoves her again, and she lashes out, swinging her arms at his face as she fights to get away from him.

"You scratched me, you bitch," he said. He touches his blurry face, and when he pulls his hands away, there's blood. "Now I'm going to make you pay."

"I'm pregnant," she says. The words stop his hand. "It's yours," she tells him. Her voice catches on a sob. "It's your baby."

I swallowed a knot that had formed in my throat.

"What did you see?" Gilly asked.

I shook my head. "I don't know. It wasn't this place." The woman from my vision was blonde. I recalled Dolly's hair had been brunette before she'd gone completely gray. Carrie was a brunette, too. But if the woman wasn't them, then who? And why was my smell-o-vision showing me an unknown female?

I leaned in for a closer look. "Do you think she fell?"

Gilly shrugged. "Possibly. I smell alcohol on her. Maybe she got drunk, stumbled, and hit her head."

My heart raced as I stepped around Dolly's lifeless form. "Poor Dolly." I shook my head. "And poor Carrie. Can you imagine trying to recover from a snake bite, only to discover your mother's died?"

"Oh, God. She'll be devastated," said Gilly.

A bruise on Dolly's wrist drew my focus. I bent over for a closer look. "It looks like someone grabbed her. The bruise is fresh. And it wasn't there yesterday. At least not that I noticed."

"I took her pulse at one point during her asthma attack. It wasn't there," Gilly agreed. "Those are definitely finger marks."

"She's got some broken nails on that hand as well." I looked around the floor and saw droplets of blood leading away from Dolly. Standing was harder than squatting, but Gilly, whose knees were much better than mine, helped me up. I gestured to the droplets. "It looks like she hurt herself somewhere else." The house wasn't any larger than my own, so it took seconds to follow the blood trace into the kitchen. A bloody mallet rested on a small butcher-block topped center island. The knot in my throat came back.

"I don't think she stumbled," I said.

Gilly took her phone from her purse and dialed 9-1-1.

CHAPTER 5

"*I* swear, Nora, you are the only person I know who keeps rubber gloves in your purse," Gilly hissed as she snapped on a pair.

"Latex," I corrected her. "And I use them for when I'm working dye through my soaps."

"If that were the case, you'd have them at the shop and not in your purse."

"I like being prepared," I said in my defense. "Though I was thinking more along the lines of soap experimentation at home. But they work for not leaving DNA at a crime scene, too."

"If you say so." Gilly looked around Dolly's kitchen. "What are we looking for?"

"For anything that might give us a clue as to who attacked Dolly. Wow. This place is really tidy for a home invasion." The butcherblock-style counters were spotless, except for a clear glass next to the sink. Coffee mugs hung on a cute pegboard near the coffee maker. Several needle point decorations that said things like *Bless the Cook* and *Faith, Family, and Food*, and *I Knead Bread* graced the walls. Even the Chinaware in the display above the stove was intact.

I noted droplets of blood on the door frame and wall near the kitchen archway, but otherwise, I didn't see any overt signs of a fight.

"Whoever hit Dolly over the head either snuck up on her, or she hadn't been afraid to turn her back on the person."

"So, she might have known whoever it was?" Gilly recoiled. "Maybe this time we should leave the detecting to the detectives." She glanced at Dolly. "Should we cover her up?"

"Better not to," I said. "We don't want to be accused of tampering with the scene."

"Honestly, do we even know if this is a scene?" Gilly countered. "It could have been an accident."

"The meat mallet accidentally bashed Dolly in the head then placed itself onto the center island."

"People have died in weirder ways." Gilly gave me a sour look. "I'm just saying. Maybe we should wait outside until the police and the ambulance get here."

"You're right, Gilly. You go on and wait out there. I'll be right behind you."

"You're a liar Nora Jean Black. Your pants are going to burst into flames at any moment."

"Eventually," I added. "Eventually, I'll be right behind you."

"I'll stay," she said as she followed me into the living

47

room.

The place was modestly decorated with pine paneled walls, some bookshelves, a plush cream-colored couch, a love seat and chair combo, along with a few framed nature scenes. But there was something obviously missing. I frowned at Gilly. "You know, there's a distinct lack of dolls in this place. For someone who owns a Doll Emporium, her home doesn't exactly reflect her love of collecting."

Gilly's frown mirrored my own. "I walked her in last night, and she did have dolls in the living room." She rubbed her arms. "Several of them. There was a sinister one with a harlequin outfit on, green and red, sitting in that baby rocking chair in the corner, and I swear its beady eyes followed me around the room."

"That does sound spooky." So, someone had stolen the dolls. But why? Dolly had a big-screen television above her fireplace. "They didn't take the television or anything else of value that I can see." There was a small chest-like box on the bookshelf. I carefully opened it so I wouldn't move it. Inside was a small cluster of hair tied with a red ribbon along with a small key, a gold band with the inscription, *Right Here Waiting*, and several gold medallions. The words Unity, Service, Recovery, and To Thine Own Self Be True were printed along the edge of the coins. The middle contained a triangle with numbers inside it.

"Those are recovery chips," Gilly said. "You know, for AA."

The biggest number I saw was two Xs. "She has a twenty-year coin here."

"That's commendable. Maybe her sobriety is what changed her into the woman she became."

I nodded. "I think she might have fallen off the wagon. I found a bottle of vodka in her purse yesterday when you had me search for her insurance card."

Gilly's eyes widened. "The coffee cup with the alcohol in it…"

I nodded grimly. "Yep. I don't think it was Tippi's."

"Poor, poor Dolly," my friend said with so much empathy it made me hurt. "You never know what's going on inside someone, no matter how they appear on the outside."

"But who would kill her for a few dolls? It doesn't make any sense."

"I don't know. Doll collecting is pretty cutthroat. Dolly told me once that she has a doll in her shop that's worth sixteen grand. She told me that when she'd won the auction, she'd gotten several threatening letters from other bidders."

"First, sixteen thousand dollars for a doll seems ridiculous. And second, do you think one of those collectors would have carried out the threats to this extent?"

"She told me this a couple of years ago, so probably not."

"But still. It sounds like doll enthusiasts can get… passionate about their collectibles."

"You mean like you with Beanie Babies?"

"That was the nineties," I told her, "And you promised to never bring it up." I still had a few boxes of Beanie Babies in storage, including a Princess PVC in mint condition. In the 90s, the price had gone to several hundred on the purple bear with the dangerous PVC stuffing. Today, it was worth about twelve bucks in mint condition. Ugh.

"I don't recall making that promise," Gilly said.

The sound of a siren drew my attention. I snapped off the gloves and put them back in my purse. "It looks like we're out of time."

* * *

TWO UNIFORMED POLICE were the first to arrive at Dolly's house. An Officer Williams, a tall man with narrow shoulders, and an Officer Perry, a woman in her thirties whose uniform top stretched at the middle button creating a small gap.

Officer Williams made us wait outside on the porch while he and Perry went inside to assess the scene. The ambulance arrived a minute or two later. I watched as Bob and Grant exited the vehicle.

When Bob stepped onto the porch, he gave us a startled look when he recognized Gilly and me. "Please tell me there's not another copperhead in there," he said.

"I don't carry extra poisonous snakes around with me," I said. "Once in a lifetime is enough, thank you."

His partner Grant was on his heels with a large red duffle bag full of supplies. "If I never see another snake, it will be too soon."

"Which one of you needs medical attention?" asked Bob.

"Not us." I gestured toward the house. "Though, I think she's been gone for a while." Gilly had mentioned that Dolly's skin felt cool when she'd checked her pulse.

Officer Williams came out the front door and took a deep breath. "Sorry, Bob, I can't let you go inside. The victim is deceased."

The paramedic nodded. "We'll stick around in case the coroner needs support."

Williams nodded. "Thanks."

"Do you need anything from us?" I asked. I hadn't called Pippa to let her know I would be late for work, not that it was going to be super busy on a Monday in February. Even though we had local customers, most of our business right now was in the making and the shipping of products. Still, Pippa had been emotional yesterday, and I didn't want to cause her any more distress.

Officer Perry joined her partner on the porch. "I'm sorry, Ms. Black, but we're going to need you and Ms. Martin to wait until the investigating detective arrives."

"Okay. I need to make a phone call then." I slipped my phone out of my purse and called Pippa.

"You've reached Pippa's phone," a woman said on the other end. "She's occupied right now, but I'm happy to take a message."

"Tippi?"

"Yes, that's me," she said brightly. "Who's this?"

"It's Nora," I told her. Pippa wouldn't have left her phone out for Tippi to use. Had something happened?

No. Jordy would have called me. Right? Unless something happened to him too. But no, Tippi sounded way too chipper. Cripes. Dolly's death was making me paranoid. "Why are you answering Pippa's phone?"

"She went to the bathroom, so I thought I would —Hey!"

"Give me my phone," I heard Pippa demand.

"Here. Take it," Tippi muttered.

"Hello," Pippa practically yelled. "Where are you?"

I held the phone away from my ear. Pippa sounded exhausted. "Gilly and I are at Dolly's house."

"Still? How long does it take to drop off a car?"

My pregnant bestie sounded like she was having another stressful day. I hated to add to it, but… "Dolly's dead."

I was greeted with silence.

"Hello? Pippa?"

"What's wrong?" Gilly asked.

"I think the call was disconnected," I said.

"It wasn't," Pippa answered. Her tone was much more subdued. "Did you say Dolly Paris is dead?"

"I did."

"How?"

"I'm not sure. But it looks like she was hit in the head."

"Please don't give out any information about the scene, Ms. Black," Officer Williams ordered. He was only a few feet away from me.

I walked farther down the drive. "I can't give you any more information right now."

"I heard," Pippa said, her anxiety obvious. "Does this mean you won't be coming in today?"

"I will as soon as all this is over. Pippa, are you okay? You can close up if you want. Take the day off."

More silence followed, then a heavy sigh. "I'm sorry. I'm being unreasonable. I just can't seem to help myself. Tippi stayed the night with me last night, and my nerves are frayed. I'm so sorry about Dolly. Does Carrie know?"

"The only people who know, other than Gilly and me, are you and the first responders." I glanced over at the glowering Officer Williams. "And I probably shouldn't have told you."

"I'll keep it to myself. I may love the gossip chain that goes through Jordy's coffee shop, but I know how to keep my mouth shut. If you do see Carrie today, tell her I'm sorry, and if she needs anything, let me know."

"I will. Thanks, Pippa. I'll keep you posted." I hung up as a red SUV slowed at the top of the drive and turned in.

The detective from the special investigations squad had arrived. As she exited the vehicle, I said, "Hello, detective."

Reese McKay narrowed her gaze at me. "Hello, Nora. Are you the one who found the possible victim?"

"Unfortunately." I shook my head. "It's Dolly Paris. It looks like someone hit her on the head with a meat tenderizer."

Reese raised her brows in surprise. "Dolly Paris. Sheesh, that's awful." I knew from my dad that the police only used codes to report deaths. Reese would have known it was a suspicious death, but not the identity of the victim. She pursed her lips and closed her eyes for a moment before looking at me again. "Why did you and Gilly come over here this morning? Were you worried about Dolly for some reason?" The way she said it, I could tell she was wondering if a vision had led me here.

"We were returning Dolly's car," I said. "She left it at the house yesterday. Her purse too. I set it down inside the house near the front door."

She nodded. "Tell me everything you know."

"That might take longer than you think," I said.

Reese took out a notepad and pencil. "Start from the moment you arrived here and take me all the way to the moment I pulled into the driveway."

CHAPTER 6

*B*efore Gilly and I left Dolly's, I took Reese aside and told her about the blonde woman in my vision. Without any context, though, the information was about as useful as a wet match.

Reese gave her nose a quick tap. "If you think of anything else, let me know."

"I will," I promised. Gilly gave Reese the keys to Dolly's vehicle, and we cleared out to let the police and the techs do their jobs.

"I can't believe she's really gone," Gilly said as we drove back to town. She shivered. "I was probably the last person to see her alive...other than her killer." She pivoted her knees toward me. "Do you think whoever did this was there when I dropped her at home? Could he or she have been waiting for me to leave?"

I wanted to comfort my friend by allaying her fears, but I couldn't deny the possibility. "Did she say anything last night when you dropped her off?"

"She was worried about Carrie, is all. Dolly said she'd been bitten by a copperhead when she was a teenager, and she'd had a major reaction. On top of that, she developed severe serum sickness to the antivenom, and it had taken months to recover. She told the doctor, and that's why he decided to keep Carrie for observation."

Ah, now it made sense that she'd had Carrie tested for a copperhead venom allergy. "Gils, what are the odds that particular snake ends up in Dolly's car the day before she's murdered?"

Gilly's face paled, and she blew out a breath. "Nora, you think the copperhead was a first attempt at killing Dolly?"

"Maybe. And whoever-it-was knew about Dolly's allergy to the venom. What if they were hoping she'd die in what would look like a terrible accident." I shook my head. "Or it could've been a warning. I don't know. But my gut says that snake was meant for Dolly."

"You need to tell Reese."

"She might've already come to that conclusion," I said. "But I'll mention it to Ezra."

I parked my SUV on the street outside the shop behind a blue sportscar. One good thing about it being low tourist season was the increased availability of parking spots.

"Oh, shoot. That's Frank," Gilly said as her gaze landed on the car in front of us. "I forgot to call him to reschedule his massage."

Frank Garrison, a forty-something loan officer at the Garden Cove Bank, was one of Gilly's long-time massage clients. He'd followed her over after she'd been let go from the Rose Palace Resort's spa. I looked at my smartwatch.

"It's only eight-forty-five. He hasn't been waiting that long. I'm sure Pippa talked to him already."

Scents & Scentsability was decorated in bright pastels and full of wonderful aromas ranging from fruity to floral—a bright and cheery contrast from the scene we'd left at Dolly's. However, I noticed the electronic doorbell didn't ring when we entered.

Pippa stood behind the counter, with a one-ounce scoop, a pile of small cellophane baggies, a variety ribbon roll, and four jars of our signature bath salts, Jazzy Jasmine, Lazy Lavender, Clearly Clary Sage and Eucalyptus, and Citrus Explosion.

"Hey, guys," Pippa said from behind the register. "Gilly's first client is here." She gestured with her head toward the massage rooms. Frank, decked out in a full three-piece suit and tie, was sipping on hot tea and relaxing with a lavender-scented neck warmer in the small waiting area we'd designed for Gilly's side of the business. "I turned the heater on the table for you."

Gilly gave her a grateful smile. "You are a magnificent creature, Pippa Davenport."

Pippa smiled. "I know, but it's still nice to hear."

Gilly shook her head and smirked as she headed into work. "I'll try to say it more often then."

"I'll hold you to it," Pippa called after her. She turned her smiling face to me, but her expression was strained and absent of any real joy. "What a day, huh?"

I nodded. "Already." I gestured back to the door. "What happened to the alarm bell?"

"It wasn't working when I got here. I called the electrician. We might need to order a new one, though."

I glanced around. "Where's Tippi?"

Pippa let out a noisy breath. "I sent her for coffee and scones for you and Gilly. I figured you all could use caffeine and sugar when you got in, and it was a good excuse to get her out from under my feet." She sighed. "It was either that or kill her, and with my surging hormones, I bet a good lawyer could mount a real defense."

"I can see you've given this a lot of thought."

Pippa groaned. "I'm sorry. You must be horrified and exhausted right now. I still can't believe Dolly is gone. She was a genuinely nice person. Do the police really believe Dolly was murdered?"

"Her death might have been an unintended consequence of a robbery gone wrong," I told her. Although that might not be true if the snake bite was a first murder attempt. "Gilly said dolls are missing from the living room."

I couldn't stop thinking about the small bottle of vodka I'd found in her purse. Had it been Dolly's? Maybe there was another explanation. After all, you didn't just throw away twenty years of sobriety, right? Honestly, I wasn't sure how alcoholism worked. I'd never had a problem with addiction, unless you counted my new obsession with online shopping, and I didn't. "You know, Dolly had a box of AA tokens."

"You think she had a drinking problem?"

"Unless those chips belonged to someone else. One of them was for twenty years of sobriety. Carrie's too young for that one."

"Carrie's a teetotaler," said Pippa. "The girl doesn't smoke or drink. I've always felt a sort of kinship with her, and now I understand why. Shared history of drunk parents."

"Aw, honey." I patted her hand as I thought about the vodka in the coffee cup. "I found an empty travel-sized vodka in Dolly's purse. I think the booze in the coffee cup was hers."

"What?" Pippa's eyes widened. "Well, now I feel bad for accusing Tippi."

"I can't stop thinking about those AA chips. If Dolly was in recovery, do you think she attended Jordy's meetings at the café?"

"Maybe, but they're supposed to be anonymous, so I doubt that Jordy would say one way or another."

"But since she's...you know, gone, does anonymity still apply?" I shrugged. "It's not like Jordy is a priest taking confessions."

"No," Pippa agreed. "But he takes the program seriously, and those who attend his meetings count on him to keep their confidence. According to Jordy, it's almost like a counseling session. They all know and keep each other's secrets of past sins while under the power of drink and drugs." She grimaced. "His words, not mine. But I know from personal experience that alcoholics can leave a lot of destruction in their wake."

"Your parents?" I asked.

"And Tippi." She shook her head. "I don't want to talk about them right now, though."

"Then we won't," I said. "But I'd still like to ask Jordy about Dolly."

"You didn't say anything to the police, did you? About Jordy, I mean."

"No, of course not, but if her drinking is an aspect they decide to pursue, it's not like the police couldn't find out about the meetings." I winced. "And there's Ezra. He knows about Jordy's past and his recovery. They are friends, after all."

Pippa shook her head. "Jordy trusts Ezra. I don't think he'd rope Jordy into any kind of mess."

"Not unless it mattered to the case," I agreed.

"I did hear through the Moo-La-Latte grapevine that Dolly and Marjorie got into a heated argument last week."

"Are you suggesting Marjorie bludgeoned Dolly?"

"No. I'm just offering up information."

"Do you know what the argument was about?"

Pippa sorted some fragrance samples on the counter. "Something about dolls Marjorie wanted to use in an upcoming gallery opening for an artist. Apparently, he paints portraits of antique dolls in modern situations."

"In modern situations?"

"You know, sitting at a computer desk, driving cars, that kind of thing."

"That sounds horrifying."

"It gets worse. They're velvet paintings."

"Like the poker-playing dogs?"

Pippa nodded. "Exactly like that."

"Who in the world would want to hang something like that over their couch?"

She raised her brows. "Someone into vintage modern chic?"

"You mean vintage modern creep."

"Potatoes, pa-tah-toes." She walked to the water dispenser, dropped a tea bag in a cup, and poured in hot water. "The point is, Marjorie had a fight with Dolly."

"And dolls were missing from Dolly's house." I shook my head. "It's a stretch."

"A big one," Pippa admitted.

"I'd still like to talk to Jordy."

She stirred her tea and sighed. "I know."

"I'm back," Tippi sang as she swept inside the shop carrying a drink holder with four sealed cups and a bag of pastries. "And I have brought the nectar of the gods with me. Damn, Pippa, your man Jordy sure makes a great cup of coffee."

"Don't remind me," said Pippa. "Put them on the counter." She stared at the paper cups and sighed. "I miss coffee."

"Oh, hey, Nora," Tippi said. "Bad luck finding a dead body."

"Tippi!" Pippa admonished.

Tippi frowned. "What? I'm being sympathetic."

Pippa gave me a "sorry" grimace. She gave her younger sister a hard look. "You didn't tell anyone, did you?"

"No." Tippi shook her head then shrugged. "I mean, I might have told Jordy. But he's family, right?"

I patted Pippa's clenched fist. "It's fine. People are going to find out soon enough. I hope the police tell Carrie before she hears it as random gossip."

"We should go check on her after work," Pippa said. "Just to make sure she's doing okay." Her eyes glistened as tears welled. "I can't believe she's lost her mother. She's going to be devastated."

Pippa's emotion tugged at me. I'd lost my mother and my father. My mother's death was still fresh for me, so it's the one that I felt the most acutely. However, the way my father had been taken from me, suddenly, that loss I would grieve the longest. Mostly because I was still angry I never got to say a proper goodbye. The last time I'd talked to him had been three weeks before he'd had a heart attack, and we'd talked about Mom's birthday and whether he should plant roses for her or get her a pair of diamond earrings. I'd voted for the earrings.

I couldn't remember if I told him I loved him before we'd ended the call.

"That's a good idea," I said. "Let's all go. Carrie will know about Dolly's death by then and will need the extra support."

Tippi tossed her blond hair over her shoulders and smiled brightly. "I can go with. You know...if you two don't mind me hanging out."

"Of course, you can come along," I told her.

Pippa coughed then narrowed her gaze at me.

Tippi's smile faded. "If you don't want me to go..."

Pippa sighed as she said, "I didn't say that. Yes, you can come with us. Not a big deal."

The younger Davenport sibling beamed with delight. "Excellent. Now, how can I help you all out today? I'm good for more than just a coffee run."

"Lunch is around the corner," Pippa said.

I rolled my eyes then turned to Tippi. "I could use some help unmolding soaps this morning."

"Sounds fun." She gave me a grateful smile. "Show me the way."

Jane burst through the front door. She was wearing a winter coat and clutching her purse to her chest as if it was trying to run away from her. On top of that, her angular face was red and glistening with sweat, her eyes wide and wild, and her bangs were matted.

"Call the police," she said breathlessly.

"What's wrong, Jane? What happened?"

"My shop." She clutched her purse so hard her fingers went white. "I've been robbed."

CHAPTER 7

I locked the front door and turned off the Open sign. "Are you hurt?" I asked Jane as I ushered her to a seat in Gilly's waiting area. Her hands trembled as she took the cup of tea Tippi offered her.

Beets' Treats was two shops down from Scents and Scentsability, but the stores between ours were currently empty. I imagined it was the reason Jane had run from her shop in our direction. We had probably been the first open door.

"It happened so fast. I'm alone on Mondays, and I'd stepped back into the kitchen to pull out my last batch of brownies. Two men in ski masks and trenchcoats ordered me to the ground." She let out a sob. "The one with the gun stepped on my shoulder and threatened to kill me if I didn't give them the combination to my safe. After they took all the money, they left."

"Out the back?" I asked although we might've noticed if two masked men had walked out onto Main Street.

Her watery gaze met mine as she nodded. "I was so scared they would return. I ran out of there as soon as they left."

"Oh, Jane. I'm sorry. You must've been terrified."

"I've never been robbed," she said, tears falling. "I was sure he was going to shoot me."

"The police are on the way," Pippa said. "They said Jane should stay here until they check out her store." I sat down next to Jane. "You said they were already in the back of your shop?"

She rubbed the crease between her eyes. "I never lock the back door. I go in and out of it all day, plus I get deliveries in the back."

I'd lived in a big city for too long not to lock my doors, though I know a lot of people who'd grown up in Garden Cove often left doors unlocked. But with the rash of robberies in the area, I was surprised Jane hadn't taken more care with her security.

I put my hand on Jane's shoulder. "It's okay. At least, it wasn't Friday."

She gave me a confused glance. "Why?"

"That's deposit day."

"I'm open on Saturdays, so I take my deposits to the bank on Mondays after work." She sobbed again.

After learning about the robbery at The Diamond Daisy, I'd felt sure the burglars weren't locals. But had they'd known how lax residents were about locking doors? Or were they looking for easy targets?

"Will insurance cover your loss?" asked Pippa.

She flushed and averted her eyes. "I hope so."

Pippa had insisted on us getting a crime insurance rider on our business insurance policy. It covered everything from stolen cash and counterfeit currency up to twenty-five thousand dollars. It was a little over fifty dollars a month extra, and with all the robberies happening around town, it seemed worth it. "Good," I told Jane. "That should help. I never thought we'd be dealing with masked bandits in Garden Cove."

"One was bad, two worrisome, but The Diamond Daisy was robbed yesterday. Jane getting burgled a day later is frightening. Why haven't the police caught these guys?"

"If it's the same group," Tippi said. "It could be different bad guys."

"It's not impossible," agreed Pippa. "But not likely."

Gilly opened the massage room door. We'd had it sound-proofed to give her clients total Zen during their sessions. Her eyes widened when she saw all of us congregated in her waiting area. She turned her face into the room and said, "Frank, take your time getting up," before stepping all the way out and closing the door. "What's going on out here?"

"Beets' Treats was robbed," Tippi blurted.

* * *

THE POLICE CAME for Jane about ten minutes later and took her back to her shop. They added extra patrols on the strip, but it still made me nervous about staying open after a neighboring shop was robbed.

66

Thankfully, the rest of the workday passed by uneventfully. No more bodies. No more robberies. Gilly left early for a pep rally for the Garden Cove Cavaliers' basketball team. Marco was the star forward, and Gilly was the team mom in charge of refreshments for tonight's game. After the Beets' Treats robbery, I decided we should start making nightly deposits, so Pippa was in the back going through the receipts and the bank deposit while I finished cleaning the front. There wasn't much to do after locking up, other than to run a dust mop over the floor, empty the trash, and wipe the counters down.

As I finished the counters, a sharp rap on the glass front door drew my attention. I smiled at the handsome sight of my Detective Hot Stuff, as Gilly called Ezra, standing outside on the sidewalk.

I unlocked the door for him, and my smile widened as he wrapped me in his arms.

"Hey there," I said into his chest. "What a nice surprise."

"I heard you had a busy morning." He gave my cheek a nuzzle.

"I still can't believe what happened to Dolly. It was awful," I told him.

"I bet." He tilted my head back so he could look me in the eyes. "I heard about Beets' Treats, too." His gaze flitted around the shop walls near the ceiling. "You should think about installing some cameras. I have a buddy that could get you set up with four in the front and a couple in the back. No cost on the installation."

"I hate the way they look, but you're probably right

that we need them." I thought about Jane and how upset she'd been about the cash she'd lost from her safe. She was a sweets shop. Most of her transactions were in cash. The loss was devastating, even if she had crime insurance. Who knows how long it would take for the insurance company to cover the loss? I let out a sound of frustration. "I can almost understand how things like this might happen in the busy season, but the shops around here barely make ends meet during the winter, and these jerks are making it even harder to run a small business."

He kissed the top of my head. "I know, sweetheart." He let me go. "I should get going. I have to go talk to Carrie Paris."

"She's been notified, hasn't she?" I hoped to hell someone had told her about her mother's death.

"Yes, Reese and one of the station's grief counselors went to the hospital this morning after she finished at the Paris house. The news, of course, came as quite a shock for Carrie, and the doctor gave her a sedative. He's worried about how the stress will affect her recovery. I called half an hour ago. The hospital social worker told me she was calmer now and willing to speak to me." Ezra pinched the bridge of his nose. "She's got weeks before she's fully recovered from the snake bite, and now she has to deal with the murder of her mom. It's a lot."

I remembered the way my mother's friends had banded together to help me when Mom died. There were times I felt smothered by their worry and attention. But now, when I look back on those few weeks before and after the funeral, I am so grateful that I hadn't had to make every decision on my own. "Dolly had a lot of friends in town. Me included. We'll make sure Carrie doesn't have to face any of this alone."

"You're a good woman, Nora."

I looped my arms around his waist. "Since you couldn't make it last night, why don't you come over tonight, and I'll show you how good I can be."

"I look forward to the demonstration," he said.

"Yes, please."

"Hey, Easy." Pippa used Ezra's nickname as she came out of the back. "Have you guys caught the Garden Cove Bandits yet?"

"Is that what they're being called?"

"Unless you have a better name."

"I do, but I can't use it in public," he said, grimacing. "Right, now I have to go to the hospital and talk to Carrie.

"I hope you find out who killed Dolly. I can't believe someone would murder another human being over dolls. It's ridiculous."

Ezra's eyes darkened. "What makes you think the dolls are a motive?"

"Well, Nora said dolls were missing. It makes sense, right?"

"We haven't determined any kind of motive at this point. That's why I need to talk to Carrie."

"I can't believe it's merely a burglary gone wrong," I said. "Especially if you count the copperhead as a first attempt."

My father always told me there were no coincidences

when it came to homicide. "Gilly said that Dolly had been bitten by a copperhead when she was young. She had a bad reaction to the antivenom."

"Dolly was organized to a fault. We found information about her snake allergy in her home office files. It makes finding a copperhead in her car a lot more suspicious." It felt as if Ezra were holding something back, but I wouldn't press him in front of Pippa. I loved that he shared his work with me most of the time. I had many favorite things when it came to being with Ezra, and hearing about his cases was definitely on the list. Even so, I understood that he wasn't always able to tell me everything.

"Poor Dolly," I said. "Hey, we were planning on going over to see Carrie in a bit. Is that okay?"

Ezra nodded. "You'll have to wait until after I finish with my questions, but I don't see any reason why you shouldn't visit."

"Good," I said. "Then it's settled. We'll head over after we stop at the bank." I gave him a quick kiss on the cheek. "Tell Carrie we're thinking about her. And if she's not ready for visitors, text me."

"You got it."

"Where are you parked?" I asked.

"Across the street."

"I'm finished here, so I'll walk you out." I glanced at Pippa. "I'll be back in a minute."

"I'll be here." She waved at me. "I better finish up back there before Tippi steals all the good silver."

"You guys keep silver in the back?" Ezra asked.

"She's joking," I told him.

Pippa gave me a bland look then smirked. "But am I?"

"Consider Tippi practice for the teenage years."

"She's thirty-five." Pippa's eyes widened. "I'm going to be seventy-three when my kid is Tippi's age."

Before she could travel too far down the drama-hole, I held up a finger. "I'll be right back."

Ezra held the door for me. "Hey, what happened to your bing-bong?"

"It's broken." I'd gotten used to its silence during the day. "We have someone coming to look at it tomorrow." I grasped his hand as we crossed the street. A chilly breeze ruffled my hair. "Yikes. It's getting colder out. I should have put on my coat."

Ezra took his jacket off and put it around my shoulders. "I won't keep you long."

We stood beside the driver's side of his truck, using the cab as a wind block. "You can keep me as long as you want."

He touched his forehead to mine. "Forever ought to do it."

I never knew how to respond when he said things like that, but my body always had the same reaction, racing pulse, giddiness, and the urge to jump his bones.

I pressed my palm against his chest. "You didn't seem surprised by the idea of the copperhead being a murder weapon."

Ezra nodded. "Animal control scanned the snake. It had a PIT tag. It's a passive integrated transponder chip injected under the scales in a snake's belly. It's activated when an animal passes any antenna set up to track wildlife."

"Did the conservation department tag the copperhead? Or was it a pet?"

Ezra shook his head. "It's illegal to keep poisonous snakes as pets in this state. They're also a protected species, so it's technically illegal to kill them as well. Anyhow, it belongs to a man who owns a snake habitat."

"Who?"

"Apparently, Johnny Scales."

"The guy Leila told us about? Hmm. She did say the thing looked well-fed. Did he know the snake was missing?"

"They called him, and he said he knew the copperhead had gone missing, but he figured the snake would hole up in a den somewhere until the weather warmed up. The conservation officer said that Johnny had been sure his snake would slither home when it got hungry."

"That can't be a thing." A shiver went down my spine. "So, in other words, no one was looking for the snake."

"Nope. I asked them to try and piece together Coop's movements based on tracking data. That's the snake's name, by the way. Coop."

"Did they find any data?"

"Late Sunday morning, Coop traveled fifteen miles from Johnny Scales snake farm to inside Garden Cove and then out past the Portman's on the Lake."

"Dolly's house is past Portman's." I stared at him. "Are you saying someone stole the snake, drove it all the way to Dolly's house, and put it in her car?"

"Coop arrived about twenty minutes before Dolly and Carrie were due to attend the baby shower. Maybe the original intention was to put it in her house, but for some reason, the car became an easier option."

"Lots of people are in the habit of starting their cars and leaving them in the driveway to warm up."

"My thoughts exactly, and a question I plan to ask Carrie," said Ezra. "It could have slithered under the console where the heater kept it warm, and they wouldn't have known it was there even as they drove to your house. After the car started to cool off, Coop could've dropped down, looking for warmth."

"And Carrie went out to the car and got the shock of her life." I shuddered, thinking about the slithering reptile lying in wait. The evidence might be circumstantial, but there was one fact that couldn't be disputed.

Coop the copperhead wasn't the only snake in town.

CHAPTER 8

*a*fter Pippa and I took the deposit to the bank, we headed to Moo-La-Latte. The deep, earthy aroma of roasted coffee beans, the sweet scent of vanilla, and the zest of chai spices hit me the way it always did when I walked into the coffee shop—like a warm hug from someone who smelled like they'd been baking all day. Fifties rock and roll played softly through the café. Pippa told me that Jordy said that fifties rock and roll was the only music he could play in the store that no one complained about. Even the country music lovers didn't mind Chuck Berry every once in a while.

Jordy, who had his long hair in a loose man bun today, was mixing a frothy drink on the other side of the bar. He hadn't shaved the sides of his head in a while, so there was an inch of growth over the tattoos on the sides of his scalp. He smiled when he saw us. "I'll be right with you all."

Pippa waddled around to where he was working. He

dipped down and gave her a quick kiss as he took the drink off the frother and set it down. "Hey, babe. Kevin's running late, but we'll get out of here as soon as he gets here."

The two of them, upon comparison, were total opposites.

Jordy had come from a working-class family in Minnesota. He was tattooed from head to toe. His body art was a combination of American traditional and neo-traditional images visible on his neck and arms. I only knew the styles because he tried to explain the differences to me. He had so many different images. Most of them tied together with open roses, skulls, and vines, but the largest tattoos that I could see were the owl that dominated his right upper arm and a phoenix on his left that stood for wisdom and rebirth. Jordy, who had been sober for more than twelve years, told me that at the beginning of his recovery, a lot of his ink had gotten him through the worst times in his recovery. Because of Jordy, I knew sobriety was a daily struggle. He said those first months had too many days where he'd found it near impossible to say no to getting high or drunk.

On the other hand, Pippa had been born into a rich family in Illinois and, as far as I knew, didn't have a single tattoo on her. I'd been surprised to learn about her family's wealth. When she'd come to work for me at Belliza Beauty, we'd connected instantly. She was the kind of woman who knew how to get things done. She had studied economics and politics at Sarah Lawrence College in New York for a couple of years before quitting and moving to Kansas City. She'd started as an intern at Belliza, and I'd seen firsthand how hard she worked. When I was promoted to regional sales manager for the company, hiring Pippa as my assistant had been the easiest decision to make. Honestly, I'm not sure what I would do without her.

Anyhow, on paper, Jordy was rough to Pippa's polish, but in reality, they were kindred spirits. They both understood what it was to want to leave a toxic past behind, and together, they'd created the family they'd been missing.

"Do you guys want something to drink?" Jordy asked. "Nora? A chai latte to go?"

"Absolutely." I was waiting for Ezra to text me about Carrie, so we had some time to kill. I sat at the closest table, and Tippi plopped down next to me.

She leaned her head back and sighed. "I would kill for a double whip mochaccino with extra chocolate sprinkles," she said loudly.

Jordy grinned. "Coming right up, little sis."

Pippa made a face, but Jordy tilted his head sideways and kissed her cheek. Her frown didn't exactly turn upside down, but I could see she was fighting not to smile. "Go get off your feet. I'll bring you some lemon and honey tea."

"I'd prefer something with more caffeine," she said.

"No coffee, love of my life. Besides, the doctor said—"

Pippa put her finger up as her eyes flickered in my direction. "Fine. I'll take the lemon and honey. Don't fuss."

When she joined us at the table, she gave me a hard stare and said, "Don't start with me."

"Oh, you wish. I am so starting with you. What did the doctor say?"

"Nothing too major," she replied.

I narrowed my gaze. "*Pippa.*"

"Fine." She threw up her hands. "She said my blood pressure was a little high, is all. Not so high as to be worried about preeclampsia, but she wants me to watch what I'm eating, increase my lean protein and decrease my caffeine intake. Like giving up coffee for this baby wasn't hard enough."

"Are you worried?"

"No." She fidgeted with the napkin she pulled from a dispenser in the middle of the table. "Maybe."

"Pip, why didn't you tell me?" Tippi asked. "I wouldn't have brought those gas station donuts home last night."

Pippa cast her sister a look of betrayal. "That was supposed to be between us."

I chuckled.

Pippa turned her stricken gaze at me as she rested her hands on her stomach. "Baby Davenport-Hines wants what Baby Davenport-Hines wants."

"So, it's the baby's fault?" I asked.

The corner of her mouth tugged up into a smile. "Yes." She tossed the napkin at me. "That's the story I'm sticking with."

Moo-La-Latte was empty, except for one customer. Davis Meadows, Marjorie's son, sat at the table in the back near the bathrooms. It was a crappy location in the coffee shop, but it had the closest access to an outlet for charging phones and such. Davis had a laptop plugged in and open in front of him as he sipped the frothy coffee Jordy had delivered. Davis was in his forties, and he was handsome in a math or science teacher kind of way. A sharp nose, glasses, and a slender physique that screamed, "I run marathons."

Okay, his mother had told me about the marathon running, but he did look fit all the same. It was strange that he'd barely looked up from his computer, even when we arrived. Whatever he was doing kept his entire focus.

Tippi noticed me staring and leaned over and whispered, "He was here this morning," she said. "Same spot, same look of intense concentration on his face. Do you know who he is?"

I nodded. "You remember Marjorie from the party yesterday?"

"The one who owns the art gallery?"

"It's her son," I told Tippi. "Davis."

"Her son can hear you," Davis said from his table. His gaze pivoted up from the screen to our table. He smiled. "Sorry. I couldn't help myself." He closed the laptop. "How are you doing, Nora? Mom says you bought a new house."

"Earlier in the year," I said. "It's right next door to Gilly's house."

He chuckled. "That doesn't surprise me one bit. Mom always says you two are peas in a pod." His thick brows furrowed as his eyes darted around the shop. "Where is Gilly?"

"She had a pep rally at the high school."

"Oh, that's right. Basketball season is in full swing." He stood up and packed his laptop into a satchel. "I better get going. I'm helping Mom design a website for the gallery along with auction links for ArtsStarts.net and AuctionArtsy.com, two of the biggest sellers online. I've finally convinced her to modernize, but I came here to work. At the gallery, she doesn't stop hovering."

While he sounded annoyed, he also sounded like a man who loved his mother very much. "I'm sure she's grateful for the help."

"I didn't know you designed websites, Davis," Pippa said. "Maybe when you're done with your mother's, you can look at ours. It took me a minute to convince Nora, but now I have her on CraftTube and Clicktock with some how-to videos. She's starting to develop a decent following."

Davis grinned, displaying his slightly crooked front teeth. "Looks like Garden Cove has its own superstar."

"A few thousand viewers don't exactly scream celebrity," I countered. Although, I had met one of my fans, Blanche Michaels, back in August. Blanche had been one of the coordinators for the beauty convention we'd attended, and she'd nearly died trying to help us solve a murder. I'd felt guilty and obliged to stay in touch with Blanche after her hospital stay. Still, Blanche's kindness and pleasant attitude had turned an obligation into a real friendship. "But I've embraced the idea of using the internet to promote the shop."

"Exactly. And Mom needs to do the same." He walked

over to the table. "You know as well as I do that money trickles in during the off-season. Last year, Gilly's tours helped us get through winter, but since she's no longer at the Rose Palace Resort, no one has taken over what she started."

"Well, I wish you guys all the luck with the website. I hope it gets you a bunch of sales."

His expression pinched. "I'd take any at this point."

I recalled my conversation about the creepy doll art with Pippa earlier. "I hear Marjorie has a new talent she's showing this month."

Davis shook his head. "It takes all kinds, that's for sure. Her partner talked her into showing this guy's stuff."

"It's not good?"

"I'm sure there's some weird...Uhm," he pushed his glasses up the bridge of his nose, "...art collectors out there willing to spend money on velvet paintings of porcelain dolls having video chat meetings." He patted his satchel. "Better get going. I told Mom I'd give her a ride home." He looked at his watch. "Shoot. I'm really late."

He left the coffee shop, and Pippa turned to me. "Aha. I told you about the doll paintings. And Davis all but admitted Marjorie needs the money."

"So she killed a fellow business owner and stole the dolls to display at her art gallery? Really?"

"Well, maybe not. But you know, if it wasn't for Nurse Mary's chain of clinics, we'd be having a tough winter as well. And Jane had talked about how hard it had been for Beets' Treats, too."

"But it does seem odd that we're having a rash of break-ins in town when businesses are struggling to meet ends."

I glanced over at Tippi, whose lower lip appeared to be jutted in a pout. "Do you have anything to add?" I asked.

"I can't believe you guys didn't introduce me to your friend." She got up from the table. "It's like I'm not even here." On that, she marched back toward the bathrooms.

"Wow. It's like she's a seventeen-year-old inside a thirty-five-year-old's body." Pippa sighed. "Same ol' Tippi."

My phone buzzed with a text message from Ezra.

Carrie would like to see you. Alone.

CHAPTER 9

*B*etween my mom's illness, my hysterectomy, and getting shot in the leg last year, I'd seen the inside of the Garden Cove Memorial Hospital enough to know my way around the place. Ezra had texted that Carrie was in the ICU, Room 6. He didn't go into why they transferred her from the medical ward for observation to intensive care, but I figured I'd find out once I got there.

I bypassed the information desk and headed to the east elevators. The ICU was on the second floor. I'd spent a few nights on the lounge chair in the waiting area while Mom had recovered from a bout of pneumonia four months before she died. She'd gotten both the pneumo-coccal vaccines at her doctor's suggestion. Still, chemo-therapy was hard on the immune system, and mom had gotten sick anyhow. The nursing staff had brought me blankets, red gelatin, and vanilla ice cream.

When she'd recovered enough to go home, I'd sent

them the largest fruit basket I could order without breaking the bank.

I depressed the intercom button.

"Who are you here to see?"

"Carrie Paris," I said. "Room six."

The door unlocked, and I went in. Instantly, I was hit with the scent of industrial cleaner, bleach, and a sickly sweetness that always reminded me of illness. Unfortunately, a lot of strong, heartbreaking memories were attached to these types of scents, and I was hit with several visions at once. I braced myself against the wall and held my breath, trying to clear the painful images.

"Nora!" A short, gray-haired nurse with big round glasses with pink frames that matched her pink scrubs waved at me. "What are you doing here?"

"Melinda." I recognized her right away. She'd been my mom's favorite nurse. "It's so nice to see you."

"You, too," she said. Her bright smile faded. "I was sorry to hear about your mom."

The visions had tapped me out emotionally, so I deflected from having to discuss Mom. "I'm here to see Carrie Paris. She was bitten by a snake yesterday."

"Oh, yes, her." She squinted and shook her head. "Are you family?"

"I'm a family friend."

"She's in a real mess today," she said in a loud whisper. The same whisper people used when they said things like, "cancer." "Is she expecting you?"

"Yes. She asked to see me." *Alone.* Why alone? I was about to find out.

Melinda checked in on Carrie to ensure she wasn't getting any kind of treatment before sending me down the hall. The ICU had a circular design with the nurse's station in the center and the room numbers ascending from the right. Room 6 was toward the back of the ward. The door was open, but I knocked anyway.

The head of Carrie's bed was elevated. She turned to me. Her eyes were red-rimmed, her skin pale, and her dark hair unruly. A bandage covered her right forearm, but her fingers, the size and look of grilled bratwursts, were poking out at the end.

"Ouch," I said. "That looks really painful."

Carrie shifted her weight and winced. "The pain meds they give me are barely touching it." She curled the fingers of her left hand. "Come on in."

I hadn't realized I was still hanging in the doorway. I walked over to her bedside and sat down in a chair situated on the left side. I lowered my gaze. "I'm so sorry about your mom, Carrie."

A choked sob caught in her throat, and tears dripped down her cheeks. "Damn it. I thought I was cried out."

I reached out and covered her non-sausage hand with mine and gave her a sympathetic squeeze. "I won't tell you it gets easier." At least for me, the pain had lessened with time. However, telling someone who just had their heart ripped out that they won't always feel this bad was condescending and unproductive. "I hope you know I'm here for you."

"I can't believe someone broke into her house and killed her." Her voice was hoarse as she fought to stop crying. "What kind of monster would do that to my mom?"

"I wish I knew." I gestured to her injured arm. "What's going on there? It looks a lot worse than yesterday."

"My arm ballooned last night, and they had to slice open the skin and muscle to relieve the pressure. The bite had caused something called compartment syndrome. They moved me to the ICU to keep a close watch to make sure it didn't spread. Or something like that. My arm hurts, but my fingers are numb. The doctors are worried that the nerves could be damaged. They have me on steroids, and they're just waiting to see what happens next." She lowered her head as the tears started again. "I want my mom."

"Oh, honey. I know." I got up and carefully put my arm around her shoulder. "I know."

A child sets the table: two plates, two forks, and two glasses of water. I can't see the child's face. Maybe eight or nine if going by size, but it's difficult for me to tell if it's a girl or a boy. The hair is shoulder length, a light caramel brown, with a choppy shag cut.

It might be Carrie's memory, or it might be the memory of one of a dozen other people who stayed in this ICU room.

The child goes to the stove and steps up on a stool to reach a small frying pan on the burner. I recognize the pegboard on the backsplash. It has different mugs, but this is Dolly's kitchen.

"Mom," the child says. "I made cinnamon toast." She carefully dumps the fried pieces of bread onto the plates. "Extra cinnamon."

When her mother doesn't come, she slides the pan back onto the stove. She walks out of the kitchen to the living room. A woman in a house dress with mousy brown hair is lying on the couch.

"Mamma." The child shakes the woman's shoulder. "It's time to eat."

"In a minute, darling," the woman replies. Her words are slurred. "Mamma needs more rest."

The child picks up an empty bottle near the couch and carries it away.

I blinked rapidly as the ICU returned, and Carrie was staring at me with concern.

"Are you okay, Nora?" she asked. "You zoned out for a moment."

I flushed guiltily. Worrying about me was the last thing the girl needed right now. "Don't fret yourself about me." I gave her a sympathetic pat before I let her go.

Carrie shook her head. "You smell like cinnamon. It's nice."

Ah, that was why the cinnamon toast memory. I slid off the bed to a stand. I wanted to ask her if she knew her mom might have started drinking again, but it would have been insensitive to bring it up just to satisfy my curiosity.

Instead, I asked, "Carrie, was there a reason you wanted to see me alone?"

She looked away for a moment and stared out the window. "I don't know if I could handle a lot of people right now." She turned back to me and met my gaze. "Do you still have my ring?"

I frowned. "I put it in your mom's purse before we took it to her house this morning, and the police took her bag into evidence."

"Why? You had it. It wasn't at her house when she—" Carrie's stare went to a far-off place. I couldn't tell if it was grief or anxiety that pinched her expression, but finally, she nodded. "Okay."

"I think they just want to check to see if anything inside the purse can point them in the right direction. I can see if I can get the ring back for you. The police usually return personal items to the family when it doesn't have a bearing on the case."

"Just leave it. I can wait." Her lower lip quivered. "What am I going to do?"

It was a good question. One without any easy answers. "You'll take things one second at a time until you stop counting seconds."

She grabbed a tissue with her good hand, blew her nose, then made a pained sound. The forceful blow must have jostled her bad arm.

"I'll let you get some rest," I told her. "I can stop by tomorrow if you want."

Carrie nodded again. "I'd like that."

I left the ICU and headed to the elevators. I got another text from Ezra.

Can you come over to my house tonight? I'll make dinner.

I wasn't about to turn down a meal I didn't have to cook.

Absolutely, I texted back. An eggplant, taco, and firework emoji were returned. I grinned and texted, *Now I want tacos.*

We'll both have tacos, he replied.

I was so busy looking at my phone that I walked right into someone as they exited the elevator. I startled back. "I am so sorry. I wasn't paying attention."

"I saw that," the young man said. I was surprised to notice it was young, good-looking EMT Grant. He smiled at me. "Hey, we keep running into each other."

"Literally, this time," I said. "I almost didn't recognize you out of uniform."

In my head, Gilly said, "That's what she said."

I chuckled. "Are you visiting someone?"

He nodded toward the ICU. "I wanted to check in on Carrie."

"Oh, do you guys know each other well?"

"A bit," he said without elaboration. "I better get in there before visiting hours are over. See you later, ma'am."

"I hope there's not a reason to see you later," I said.

His brow lowered for a moment, then he laughed. "Oh, yeah. Right."

I got on the elevator before he got to the ICU doors, but I was less concerned with the young EMT and more focused on eggplants, tacos, and fireworks.

CHAPTER 10

I went home to shower and change into more comfortable clothes before driving over to Ezra's place. He lived in a small two-bedroom cabin off Lake Access Road V outside of Garden Cove. There was a path behind his house that led to a small boat dock on the lake. Thinking about the last time we'd gone down there for a moonlight swim made me wish for summer.

Ezra was younger than me, but we matched up where it counted the most. We loved each other. Our conversations were always easy and interesting. We both had similar ideas about family and friends, and the passion between us remained intense. I'd never been happier in my life.

Ezra sat in a rocking chair under his covered porch wearing a red and black flannel shirt and faded blue jeans. The sexy half-smile on his lips as I walked up the steps to him was so much hubba-hubba.

As I closed the distance between us, he reached out and pulled me onto his lap. "Hey there."

I laughed as I looped my arms around his neck. "Hey."

He rested his face on the divot of my shoulder. "I've been looking forward to this moment all damn day."

I cupped his face with my hand. "Me too."

He kissed my palm. "You always smell so damn good."

"Luck of the trade," I told him. I'd been unmolding and packaging scented soaps all day long. The last batch had been warm cinnamon and vanilla.

"Luck of the boyfriend." He nuzzled my neck and slid his hand under my jacket. "Dinner's done, by the way. But it's just as easy to warm it up later."

"I'm good with a reheat."

Ezra slid his hand behind my neck and tilted his head back to meet my gaze.

God, I loved the way he looked at me.

He kissed me, his firm lips commanding my attention as his velvet tongue swept mine. He tasted of spearmint, which meant he'd popped a mint before going outside to wait for me. I moaned as he unzipped my jacket and pushed up my shirt.

The evening had dropped the temperature down into the forties. I stopped him just short of sliding my coat off. "Maybe we should take this inside."

Ezra chuckled. "If that'll get your clothes off faster."

"It certainly will." I slid off his lap to stand.

When he got up, he put his hand on my hips, grinned, then hoisted me over his shoulder.

"Ezra!" I grabbed onto his back to keep from falling.

"I've got you," he said, planting his hand firmly on my ass. "And I don't plan on letting you go."

It was a promise I clung to as he carried me into the house and back to his bedroom. We made love until we both collapsed from exhaustion.

Ezra rolled to his back, and I curled up against his chest.

He blew out a ragged breath. "Wow. That thing you did with your tongue, you know, the reverse thing."

"I know the thing you're referring to," I said with a laugh. Gilly had been schooling me on different things to try out, and I was the kind of student who paid attention.

He chuckled low and sexy as he curled his arm around me, drawing me closer so he could kiss me. "That was something real special, darling."

"I'll put it on the list of things you really like."

"When it comes to you, Nora Black, that's a really long list."

"Back at you, Ezra Holden."

He lazily stroked my hair as we lay naked and tangled together for a few moments of blessed silence. "What a way to start a day, huh?"

"If that's your way of saying you want to talk about what happened to Dolly, I'm okay with it."

"Did you get any of your aroma mojo at the scene?"

"I saw a blonde woman fighting with a man. She said they weren't supposed to use guns and that someone was dead because of the guy. He pushed her. She scratched his face. But that's it. A big fat load of nothing helpful."

"Do you think the woman was Dolly?"

"Honestly, I don't know. But I don't think so. Maybe the vision was of the killer and someone else."

"You think the man in the vision killed Dolly?"

I slid my hand over his chest. His chest hair was cool against my warm fingers. "Maybe. Or maybe the woman. Or both. Or neither." I sighed. "I don't know."

"She said something about a gun?"

I nodded. "Has anyone been shot around here lately?"

"No, but Jane Beets and Dan Briggs both say that they were robbed at gunpoint."

"And the jewelry store?"

Ezra shook his head. "No gun that the owner saw. It was a fast and efficient smash and grab."

"But in all three robberies, the thieves wore ski masks and trenchcoats, right?"

"Witnesses have issued the same descriptions, yes."

"Do you think the thieves are getting sloppy?"

"Maybe. Or it's a different duo altogether." The tension in his face deepened the lines on his forehead. "I suspect we have two sets of robbers, which means looking at the evidence in a new way." He rubbed his face. "I feel like I've been shaking all the wrong trees for oranges when I should be searching for nuts."

"What about the dolls that were stolen from Dolly's house?"

"That's another tree entirely, I think," Ezra said.

I chuckled. "I mean, did you ask Carrie about them? If they were worth any money or if she had any idea why someone would take them?"

Ezra tucked his chin at me. "You mean you didn't ask her?" He made it a question.

"Oh, believe me, I wanted to before I got there, but that girl is having one of the worst days of her life. I couldn't bring myself to grill her about her mom."

Ezra caressed my shoulder. "You're a kind woman."

I gave him a lazy smile. "I don't know about that, but I'm not without sympathy. Especially when it comes to the loss of a parent."

"Carrie didn't have a lot of current information about her mom. She said Dolly had been distant for weeks, avoiding phone calls, and that she had canceled two dinners as well. She'd been surprised when her mother agreed to go to Pippa's baby shower."

"Carrie doesn't live with Dolly anymore, does she?"

"No, she moved out in December of last year."

"Before Christmas?"

He nodded.

"Ouch." I shook my head. "Did she say anything about the dolls?"

"She said that there were nine dolls in the living room and five in Dolly's bedroom that were extremely precious to her mother. Carrie wasn't even allowed to touch them when she was growing up, so she guessed they were valuable." He sighed. "Carrie said that Dolly keeps a master list of her collection in a file cabinet at her office. She gave us permission to search Dolly's business, which saves us a search warrant."

"Do you have the shop key? Or are you guys going in

SWAT-style?" I glanced up at him. "Because you and a battering ram could be super hot."

"I'll bring home the battering ram tomorrow night."

I snorted a laugh. "You bring home a battering ram every night."

Ezra's eyes widened, then he started laughing, which made me laugh some more, and in a few minutes, our laughs verged on hysteria. Both of us had tears in our eyes, and we were struggling to breathe, and it took a few false starts before we were finally able to talk again.

"I haven't laughed that hard in a long time," Ezra said.

"Me either. We must have needed it." A shadow of a bare tree branch bounced along his wall as the wind picked up outside. It reminded me of a snake. "That was strange about the copperhead. Are you guys investigating whether someone stole the snake and put it in Dolly's car? Or had she gone to visit Johnny Scales, and it just crawled in there on its own? Gilly said that Dolly had gotten bitten when she was young. I can't imagine someone with that kind of history voluntarily visiting a bunch of snakes, though."

"I'm taking Dolly's picture over there tomorrow afternoon." He tipped my chin up. "Do you want to come with me?"

My pulse picked up a beat, mostly because I seriously wanted to go. "I would love to, but are you sure it's a good idea?"

"You've worked as a consultant for us several times now, and I'd love to employ your talents to see if you pick up any vibes at the snake farm. Besides, from what I hear, Johnny Scales is quite the character, so it will be fun to experience him for the first time with you."

"A work date, huh?"

"A cheap date," he teased.

"Always cheap," I smirked. "But never easy."

"And I'm always easy, but never cheap." He chuckled. "Who am I kidding? I'm cheap as hell."

I crawled up his chest and kissed him. "Got that right, mister."

"Let's get lunch first, then snakes."

"You got it," he said. "And speaking of food. I've got pork simmering in the crockpot for carnitas and a mess of corn tortillas in the warmer."

"Did you make fresh pico?"

"Of course," he said. "Extra spicy."

I sighed happily. "You really do love me."

He kissed me again. "I really do."

CHAPTER 11

The next morning, Gilly didn't show up for our usual coffee-before-work ritual. I walked over to her house and knocked on the door. Ari, Gilly's teenage daughter, answered. She'd been letting the top of her hair grow out, and recently, she'd shaved the left side.

"Morning, Aunt Nora," she said. "Mom's upstairs in her room."

"Is she sick?"

Ari's eyes were the color of expresso, a deep, dark, and rich shade of brown. Her father, Gilly's ex-husband Gio, was one-hundred percent Italian. Both Ari and her twin Marco had his coloring.

She grabbed my arm and tugged me inside. "You better go up and see for yourself."

Even though my knees hurt less, I still didn't love going up, and down the stairs, just in case the old pain flared up. But for my girl Gilly, I risked it.

I knocked on her closed bedroom door. "Gilly?"

"Don't come in, Nora." Her tone was despondent. "I'm hideous."

"Even if you've managed to grow a third eye overnight, you'd be gorgeous," I said.

Ari stood behind me and snickered.

I gave her what I hoped was a withering stare.

The seventeen-year-old did not wither. Not one bit.

"I'm coming in," I said with my hand on the door handle.

"You're going to laugh."

"I won't laugh."

"You can't know that, Nora. Because if it was you, I'd laugh."

I glanced at Ari. "What happened?"

She shook her head.

I turned the handle. "Brace yourself." I opened the door and went into the bedroom. A Gilly-sized lump moved under a pale peach down comforter on her king-sized bed. "What are you doing?"

I'd bought the down comforter for her, so I knew it was also weighted. Her voice was muffled under its thickness. "Hiding my shame."

"Did you shave your head?"

"No." The stricken note in Gilly's tone told me I'd hit close to home. The morning before, she had shown up with homemade highlights. She hadn't liked them, but I thought they'd looked cute.

"Come on, Gilly bear," I said, resorting to my high school nickname for her. "It can't be that bad. Besides, who always has your back?" I pointed to myself even though she couldn't see me. "Nora Black, that's who."

"I can't even with you two," I heard Ari say from the hall. Then she yelled, "Marco! If you're not ready in two minutes, you can take the bus to school."

"Marco's not driving himself?" I asked.

Gilly, still muffled from the blanket, said, "He's grounded."

"For what?"

"Fighting." She threw the cover off her, revealing a shocking amount of silvery gray hair mixed in with a caramel brown. "He's been suspended from the basketball team for three games as well. He tackled a guy. He's lucky he didn't get suspended from school, too."

I focused on her words as I fought back my horror at her hair. Frankenstein's bride had nothing on my BFF. "Why did he tackle a guy?"

"Because the dude clocked me in the face with his elbow," Marco poked his head in the room. "I don't know why you're so pressed about it." His nose was swollen, and the area below his right eye was purple. The kid was blessed, though. Even battered, he was cute.

"Because violence is a terrible way to solve your problems," Gilly told him.

He sucked his teeth then gave me the nod. "Hey, Aunt Nora."

"It looks to me like the guy deserved to be tackled," I said.

Marco smiled and patted the door. "See," he said to

his mother. "Aunt Nora gets it." We fist-bumped with a little blow-up at the end.

Gilly glared at me. "Don't encourage him." She snapped her fingers in his direction. "Go to school."

He made a kissy face at his mom before taking off down the hall to the stairs. I refocused my attention on Gilly.

"That boy. He's been unpredictable lately," she said.

I raised a brow at her and stared pointedly at her gray-streaked hair. "He's not the only one."

She grabbed her hair with both hands. "It's awful, isn't it?"

"I don't know," I answered. She'd told me before she was interested in letting her natural gray grow out. Now that I saw her with the color and gotten over the initial shock, it really didn't look too bad. "Is that the color you were going for?"

"It was not. It was supposed to be a color lifter with a demi-gloss to add the color Downtown Brown to my hair." She let out a noise of frustration. "But instead, I ended up with Clowntown Gray. I looked it up on the internet, and several reviews said this happens when you try to put this color over bleached hair." She buried her face in her hands. "Oh, Nora, why didn't I read the reviews first?"

"It's...uh, flattering." Sorta. Maybe if we styled it a different way, or...Gilly could wear a nice hat. Or I could make an emergency hair appointment with Rita at the Curl Up and Dye.

She pivoted her gaze to meet mine. "Really?"

"No," I admitted. I pulled my phone out of my jacket pocket. "I'm calling Rita, and we're going to fix this."

"I told her to do that already," Ari yelled right before the front door slammed shut.

"That kid has the ears of a bat," I said.

"You're not kidding," Gilly agreed. "I have to go out to the car anytime I want to have phone sex with Luke."

I barked a laugh.

Gilly smirked. "You said you wouldn't laugh."

"At your hair," I said. "Your love life is fair game."

My BFF, wearing pink satin pajamas, climbed out of bed. "We can't all be dating Mr. Perfect."

"That's Detective Perfect," I corrected. "Ezra has his faults."

"Like what?"

"He hangs the toilet paper backward. It makes it difficult to unroll."

"You're right," Gilly said. "He's a monster."

"Flawed," I corrected.

"Does he know any more about what happened to Dolly? Have the police got any suspects or leads?"

"He's going to search the Doll Emporium this morning, then this afternoon he's taking me to Johnny Scales' snake farm."

"Fancy," Gilly said sardonically but with a smile. She retrieved underwear from her dresser. "Give me twenty minutes to shower and throw on some clothes, and I'll be ready to go."

"Sounds like a plan."

* * *

WITH GILLY safely in Rita's hands, I went to work. She still hadn't arrived by the time I left Scents and Scentsability for my lunch date with Ezra. I wondered how much magic Rita had to work to fix my BFF's hair snafu.

"Nora!" Marjorie Meadows, wearing a pearly white winter peacoat over cream-colored dress pants, waved from across the street. "Yooo hooo," she added with another furious wave.

Ezra nudged me with his shoulder. "I think Ms. Meadows wants to talk to you."

I waved back to the woman. "I see her," I said out the side of my mouth. Louder, I called out. "Hey, Marjorie. Hold up, and I'll come to you." I nudged Ezra back. "Come on."

"I'll go warm up the truck."

"It's fifty degrees outside. You're good," I said.

He shook his head but smiled.

"Detective Holden," Marjorie said breathlessly as if she'd been jogging. "Always so good to see you."

He dipped his head. "Thank you, Ms. Meadows. It's good to see you too."

She flushed with pleasure. I could see now that she was holding a short stack of flyers. Marjorie plucked a sheet off the top and thrust it at me. "I hope you can make it to the showing I'm having on Friday. The artist, Christopher Staten, is so unique in the way he combines contemporary and retro mediums to create a new kind of pop art. He's practically the Andy Warhol of the Midwest."

Ezra snorted a laugh then coughed to cover it. I gave him a quick elbow to his side and hid my smile.

"Why that sounds like so much fun, Marjorie. Of course, Ezra and I would love to come to your new show."

"Wonderful." She clapped her hands, and a few of the flyers flitted to the sidewalk.

Ezra picked them up.

"You're such a gentleman, Detective Holden." She flashed him a smile. "Someone raised you right."

Ezra's mother had died when he was in high school. A year later, he'd gotten his high school sweetheart pregnant. Losing his mom and having a child all by the age of sixteen had forced Ezra to grow up fast.

Still, he gave Marjorie his most charming smile back and said, "Someone did."

Marjorie's expression darkened as she touched my hand with her fingertips. "I heard about Dolly Paris. What a tragedy," she said. Her eyes lowered before flickering back up to meet my gaze. "I heard you and Gillian found her."

I nodded because it would've been pointless to deny it. "It's terrible," I agreed.

Marjorie's fingers curled around my wrist. "Are there any suspects?"

Aside from you? I brushed the thought away. I couldn't see Marjorie killing anyone for a good reason, let alone a bad one like Dolly not lending her some dolls.

Ezra answered. "We're pursuing multiple avenues on the case right now, but nothing I'm allowed to talk about. You understand." When Marjorie nodded, he added, "Do you know of anyone who would've wanted to harm Dolly?"

"I…" Her eyes got that far-off look in them for a second, then she nodded. "She got into a fight with Carrie about a new boy she was seeing. Dolly didn't approve. She thought the guy was using Carrie."

"Do you know who Carrie was seeing?" I asked.

"Dolly didn't say. She just said the man reminded her of the past and that the past should stay in the past. You know how Dolly was. She could be cryptic, especially when it came to her personal life."

I'd told Ezra that Pippa had heard that Marjorie had been in a tiff with Dolly, so he pushed a little harder. "Was she fighting with anyone else? Over business," he said. "Or the like."

Marjorie shook her head. "Not that I know of."

"I heard you'd wanted to borrow some of her dolls," I blurted.

The older woman's expression curdled like spoiled milk. She narrowed her gaze at me. "What are you insinuating?"

Ezra stepped in. "Where were you two nights ago?" he asked. "Between eight and ten o'clock?"

"Am I a suspect?"

He shook his head. "No, ma'am. But you were one of the last people to see Dolly on Sunday."

"Along with all the guests at Pippa's baby shower. Are you asking them for alibis?"

Ezra smiled. "Yes, ma'am. We surely are."

"It's more for ruling out than ruling in," I added.

That seemed to mollify Marjorie. She nodded curtly. "I watched two episodes of *Bridgerton,* then went to bed."

A zip of excitement fluttered in me. "Is it good? I've heard it's like watching Jane Austen sexed-up."

"That's an excellent description," Marjorie said. She flushed again. "I'll admit, I'm rewatching the entire season." She sighed and shook her head. "I'm sorry for getting my back up about your questions. It's been a stressful month. Like everyone around here, the gallery is struggling. Davis is doing his best to extend the gallery's reach, but you know how it is."

"I do." We'd been so lucky to get the medical spa contract. "I didn't mean to come off like an interrogator."

Marjorie *pish*ed and made a swatting motion in the space between us. "I did fight with Dolly. She could be hardheaded. I thought combining some of her dolls with the artwork would have been good for both of us, business-wise. I wanted to pose them to mirror the canvases, but she flat out refused. I'll admit, I was irritated with her, but not enough to do something so heinous." She fixed her gaze on me. "You believe me, don't you?"

"I do," I said.

Ezra put his arm around my shoulders. "We better get going. We have a lunch reservation."

Marjorie forced a smile. "I hope to see you both Friday night."

As we walked back to Ezra's truck, I gave him a side-long look. "Reservations?"

"At the finest establishment in Garden Cove."

"And where might that be?"

"The Taco Shake Shack, of course."

The Taco Shake Shack was the oldest drive-thru diner in Garden Cove, and it served the best milkshakes and tacos in the state as far as I was concerned. The man definitely knew the way to my heart.

I turned into him and gave him a kiss that I hoped conveyed just how lucky I felt to have him in my life. After I said, "Gilly was right. You are fancy."

Ezra's gaze softened as the slip of a smile played on his lips. "Only the best for my girl." He gave me a quick pat on the rear and said, "First shakes and then snakes."

I pressed my hand to my chest. "Be still, my heart."

CHAPTER 12

*T*he odor in the office of Scales, Scales, and Scales smacked me in the face as we entered. It was as if a skunk, a rotting egg, and a dead body had combined into the most putrid concoction I'd ever smelled. I gagged.

"What the hell died in here?" Ezra pinched his nose.

It was undeniably potent. "I can actually taste it." The tacos and shakes began to gurgle in my tummy. Two heaters were going in the room, along with a humidifier, and it really enhanced the pungency. I opened the door to let some fresh air in.

"Christ almighty, something crawled up this snake's butt and died," a man says by an open door. He's wearing a beanie, so I can't tell what color his hair is.

"It'll be fine once she settles," a bald guy says. I can only see the back of his head as he uses gloved hands and a hook to carry a red, yellow, and black ringed snake to an open green tub. "She'll make you a really nice companion."

"It stinks. I didn't expect it to smell this bad." He waves his hand. "I change my mind. I don't want the snake."

The man with the hook turns on the guy, holding the angry snake out in front of him. He has a scraggly beard that stretches past his neck to his chest. "I've already paid to have her brought here for you. You're not getting your money back if that's what you think."

"I paid you five thousand dollars."

The bald guy laughed and thrust the snake toward the man. "You gonna call the cops?"

The backdoor to the office opened as the vision faded, and a bald man with a long, braided beard and lots of tattoos walked in. He wore skinny jeans that looked like they been used to clean up a grease spill, a tank top that was cut open under the arms, a pair of combat boots that looked as if they hadn't seen a shine in years. He waggled a finger at us. "Close the door, you damn fools. You're letting all the heat out."

He was hardly dressed for winter, but I didn't say anything as I let go of the door, and it swung closed.

The man's nose wrinkled as the stench hit him. "Lordy sakes, Petey." He waved his hand in front of his nose then cackled. "Something must have startled Petey for him to release that much musk."

I looked around the office. Other than an empty-looking screened-in cage with some branches situated in the middle, I didn't see any Petey's. I cast a startled glance at Ezra. Had we let a snake out?

Ezra frowned. I could tell he was wondering the same thing.

"Uhm, what's a Petey?" I asked.

"He's hiding up under the lid." The bearded man walked over, opened the lid, reached inside, and retrieved a three-foot red, black, and yellow ringed snake. "Here's Petey, and I'm Johnny Scales, the owner of this here zoo. Are you folks here for a tour?"

I took several steps back as the snake coiled around Johnny's wrist. "Why don't you take the lead, honey," I said to Ezra.

He smirked and shook his head. "I'll just hang back here with you for now."

"Is that thing poisonous?" I asked. It looked an awful lot like a coral snake, and I knew those were super deadly. Ever since the copperhead incident, I'd been Googling poisonous snakes.

"Petey here poisonous?" Johnny shook his head. "Not hardly. He's got killer looks, but that's about it. He's a non-venomous scarlet kingsnake, or what some folks call a milk snake. I picked him up from a dealer in Virginia a couple years back."

"He looks deadly."

Johnny scales grinned, and I could see he was missing one of his front teeth, and the remaining ones were slightly yellow and cracked in appearance. "As the saying goes, yellow on red, you're probably dead, but red on black, he's friendly, Jack." The reptile wrangler laughed again. He held up the snake again. "See, Petey has red on black, so his bite isn't poisonous. Coral snakes are the venomous ones."

Petey might have been black touching red, but in the

vision, I was sure the snake he'd been holding was yellow touching red. Was Johnny illegally selling venomous snakes to people?

Ezra coughed at the lingering scent. "And the smell?"

"He's small, but his musk is mighty. He releases it when he's scared. You all must have startled him when you came inside. I usually watch for cars pulling into the parking lot, but I was feeding the rest of my beauties." He put Petey back in his cage, dusted his hand on his jeans, and held out his hands. "That'll be ten dollars each for the tour."

I stopped Ezra with a slight shake of my head before he could introduce himself as a police detective. "Sure," I told Johnny. "That sounds fair."

Ezra gave me a questioning look, and I touched my nose and gave him what I hoped was a *go with me on this* one look back. If Johnny was selling deadly snakes, maybe he'd sold Coop to someone willing to pay.

He shrugged, then took out his wallet and produced a twenty-dollar bill. He handed Johnny Scales the money. "Let's see what you got."

Johnny Scales led us down a covered corridor across the grass that consisted of winterizing plastic and two-by-fours. "I built this to keep out as much of the elements as possible during the cold months. It cuts down on the heating bill."

Up ahead, there was a sign over a door that said, "The Slither Pit." Johnny pushed three slide bolts open, then smiled back at us. "Welcome to the pit," he said.

I felt the same nervous energy I'd had the first time I

went on a roller coaster. I wanted to ride and run all at the same time. There was no way I was taking the chicken exit, no matter how scared I might be.

However, I did grasp Ezra's arm with two hands and held on tight. He patted my wrist and smiled. "Fun date, huh?"

"So far," I told him.

The Slither Pit was wall-to-wall terrariums. Johnny grouped them into poisonous versus non-poisonous and then by color. Each habitat had a sticker in the right-hand corner that gave information about the snake enclosed.

"This is Shorty," Johnny said of a brown and reddish-brown snake in one of the larger cages. "He is a red-tail boa constrictor all the way from Peru. The males of his species are thinner and not as long as the females, but he can grow over ten feet long. Although he's already seven years old and only six feet in length, so he probably won't get that big. It's why I named him shorty."

"He seems plenty big to me," Ezra said.

"Same," I agreed. Six feet was more snake than I wanted to come up against. "Is it dangerous?"

"Nah. Not unless provoked. The red-tail make good pets because they are one of the gentler snakes out there." He cackled. "Why are you looking for something to take home? I could probably get you a deal."

I blanched. "Uhm, I might be interested in something a little more…exotic if you're selling."

Johnny squinted at me. "What do you mean by exotic?"

Ezra said, "Go ahead, sweetheart. Tell him what you mean."

"You know, something in the more lethal department." I walked over to his wall of venomous snakes. I pointed at a timber rattlesnake. "Something like this fellow." I gulped as I took in the large rattle on the end of his tale. My throat was dry as I rasped out, "Isn't he cute?"

"Adorable," I heard Ezra say.

"You all aren't cops, are you?" Johnny asked. "You have to tell me if you are."

"Nope," Ezra said. "No cops here."

I couldn't believe how many people still thought that police in plain clothes or in sting operations had to identify themselves. It simply wasn't true, but it was easier to let Johnny believe what he wanted.

"I'm not a cop," I said. "I want one of these beautiful creatures for my home terrarium. It'll make a great conversation starter."

Ezra let out a sharp snort then reined himself in. "It would be the life of the party," he added. Then to Johnny, he asked, "How much?"

"Rain there is special to me." He stroked the braid in his beard. "It's gonna hurt to part with him."

"What would it take to make it hurt less?" I asked.

"Twenty-five hundred," Johnny said without any hesitation.

"Is that how much you charged the person who bought Coop?" Ezra fished.

Johnny frowned. "How do you know about Coop?"

"Who did you sell the copperhead to?" I asked him.

"Hey, you said you weren't the police."

"I'm not," I told him.

Ezra smiled. "I'm Detective Ezra Holden, so you can answer a few questions about the copperhead you sold." He shrugged. "Or I can arrest you right now for the illegal sale of venomous snakes."

"No money changed hands, so technically, I didn't sell you anything."

"Once you named your price, you incriminated yourself," Ezra said.

I wasn't sure if that was true, but I liked Ezra's style. "Of course," he added, "You do have the right to remain silent and the right to an attorney, but once that happens, I can't help you out anymore."

"I'm just trying to make a living out here," Johnny protested. He raised his hands and started backing away from us. "You know how much it costs to feed my babies? Buying mice in bulk is expensive. I only sell a few snakes to help make ends meet. I'm not a bad guy."

"Stay where you are," Ezra cautioned him.

Johnny took another step backward until his back was against one of the glass habitats. My new Lasik eyes were great, but the sticker was too far away for me to tell what snake was in the case.

"Ezra," I warned.

He was going to his backup pistol at his ankle as Johnny unlatched the cage, slid open the glass door.

"Don't do it," I squealed as he reached back and grabbed the snake. In a flash, the thick-bodied reptile seemed to float out onto the air in a gravity-defying moment that made my stomach drop. I staggered backward as its head puffed out into a giant hood.

"Oh, God," Ezra said, yanking me behind him. "Cobra."

Johnny, holding the tail of the cobra, shouted. "I'm not going back to prison."

Suddenly, the snake turned on him and struck him on the hand. He reflexively yanked his hand back, and the snake went back into his terrarium.

"I'm bit!" Johnny held his hand against his side as he slumped to the ground. "King cobra antivenom," he said. "It's in the fridge. Hurry. I can't...it's getting harder to breathe."

I got my phone out. "Calling 9-1-1."

"Good," Ezra said. "I'll contain the snake." Ezra, his gun trained on the cobra, slid the glass door closed and latched it. "Where's the refrigerator?" he asked Johnny.

Johnny shook his head, unable to talk, much less move. Ezra took off in search of the fridge. The venom of the cobra was taking effect quicker than the copperhead's poison had on Carrie. Johnny was pale, sweaty, and his respirations were fast and shallow.

When the emergency operator answered, I said, "We need an ambulance at Scales, Scales, Scales off Highway 49, ramp 57, on the far side of Bunny's Triple X. A man's been bitten by a—" I looked at the sticker. "—a king cobra."

Johnny slumped over. "Hurry," I told the operator. "I don't think he has much time."

CHAPTER 13

"*I* swear I'm going to put 9-1-1 on speed dial," I said as I sat with Ezra on the open tailgate of his truck for the police and conservation officers to arrive.

Ezra had found a fridge under Johnny's office desk with a box of six ten-milliliter vials with white powder in them marked as antivenom for a tiger snake, but a piece of paper with the words *King Cobra* was taped to the side. There was also a couple of vials of saline. Unfortunately, neither of us knew where the syringes were or even how to administer a dose.

The EMTs arrived. They were from Rasfield, not Garden Cove. Rasfield wasn't in our county, but its emergency services and the hospital were closer to the scene. Johnny was barely breathing when they arrived, and his pulse was thready and weak. They immediately intubated Johnny and started bagging him. Since King Cobras weren't native to the area, they took the vials of antivenom powder with them. Ezra called Shawn to let him know what went down at the snake farm. Shawn told him he'd call Rasfield PD and coordinate with them on Johnny's custody if he survived.

I had my doubts. While the paramedics worked the scene, I worked Google on my smartphone.

"Did you know that it can take up to fifty doses of antivenom to counteract the paralysis caused by the neurotoxin from a king cobra snake bite?"

Ezra shuddered. "Why in the world would someone keep something so lethal?"

"And," I added, "even with the antivenom, often a victim has to be put on a ventilator so the machine can breathe for them until the paralysis in their lungs wears off."

Ezra touched his throat. "Yikes."

"And then some." I put away my phone and laced my fingers in his. "I hope he makes it. I really want to know who bought the copperhead from him."

"I'm guessing you got a vision when we got here. Tell me about it."

"He sold a coral snake, at least I think it was a coral snake, to someone for five thousand dollars. From what I could tell, the musk of a coral snake stinks just as badly as the musk of a scarlet king snake because the buyer had some serious remorse over his purchase."

Ezra chuckled. "I bet he did."

"I remembered you saying that it was illegal to buy and sell venomous snakes, so I figured Johnny was doing a little under the table dealing."

The corner of his mouth quirked up in a half-smile. "You figured right." He turned my hand over in his. "Hey, you were good in there. You'd make a decent undercover cop."

"There's only one decent cop I want to be under the covers with," I replied warmly. "But I know what you mean. Thanks. I appreciate the compliment. I'm happy you trusted me enough to go along with it."

"I do trust you, Nora. I hope you know that. I hope you trust me, too."

I gave his hand a squeeze. "I do, Ezra. On both counts."

Two conservation officers showed up at Scales, Scales, Scales after the ambulance left. They parked their brown van next to Ezra's pickup.

Ezra got up to greet them.

I recognized one of the men as Perry Porter. He'd been a year ahead of me in high school, and one of the best defensive players Garden Cove's football team had ever seen. His hair had a touch of gray at the temples, and it was thinner than it used to be, and his narrow waist had gotten thicker over the years. But his neck and arms still looked like they were built out of tree trunks. Gilly had crushed on Perry our entire junior year. I couldn't wait to tell her that I ran into him.

"Hi, Perry," I said. "Remember me?"

His light gray eyes lit up as he recognized me. "Well, hot damn, Nora Black. Wow. It's been a minute, but you still look great." He smiled, and it made his face appear years younger. "I heard you and Shawn got married," he said. "He's a lucky man." Shawn had been a year ahead of me in school as well, and he'd been an athlete, so he and Perry had palled around a bit.

"We're divorced," I said quickly.

"Too bad for Shawn. So you're single?"

Ezra's gaze fell on me as I said, "Nope. Not single either."

"I'm Detective Ezra Holden," Ezra said. "I'm in charge of the scene for now."

"Perry Porter," Perry said as he shook Ezra's hand. He gestured to the young woman who was getting equipment from the side of the van. "That's Evelyn. She's our local herpetologist." I must have looked as confused as I was because he clarified, "Snake expert."

"Gotcha," I said.

"If you'll show me the way, Detective," Evelyn said. She had short brown hair, and glasses, probably in her early thirties, and she had a large duffle bag over her shoulder. "I'll get started on categorizing the reptiles."

Ezra took her inside the building while I stayed outside with Perry.

"I'm surprised to see you in conservation. I always thought you'd go on to coach high school or college ball. You were really great."

"I always liked nature and animals, so I used my football scholarship as a way to get my environmental science degree." He nodded toward Ezra, who was coming back out of the Scales, Scales, Scales office. "Are you with the police department now?"

"No. I run a shop in Garden Cove."

"And she sometimes works as a consultant," Ezra said. He jerked his thumb over his shoulder. "Your partner asked me to send you in."

Perry gave Ezra a friendly salute. "Better go then." He winked at me. "It's nice to see you again, Nora. We should catch up sometime."

He took off before I could formulate an answer.

Ezra stared at me, then laughed. "You look like a deer caught in the headlights."

"I feel like one."

He dug his keys out of his pockets. "Why don't you take my truck? I'll get a ride from one of the patrols after I finish up here."

I was getting antsy to go. "You don't mind?"

"Are you kidding? I don't want to give Perry another pass at my girl," he teased.

"You don't have anything to worry about," I said.

"I'm glad." He placed the keys in my hand. "But there's no reason for you to stick around. There's still a couple of hours' worth of stuff to do here. If we find anything interesting, I'll fill you in when I pick up the truck."

"It sounds like we have a plan."

* * *

GILLY WAS at the shop with Pippa, and her hair looked fabulous. She patted her new glossy brunette locks with golden highlights. "Better?"

"You look like a million bucks." I hugged her. "Maybe you should stick with Rita when it comes to hair color."

"She agrees with you," said Gilly, laughing.

I filled in Pippa, Gilly, and Tippi on my lunchtime adventure.

"A king cobra?" Pippa gasped. "Oh my gawd, Nora. That sounds terrifying."

"I almost peed my pants," I admitted. The store was empty of customers, and we were all gathered around the counter.

"A sneeze makes me pee my pants, lately," Pippa said.

Gilly laughed. "Pippa probably would have shot that baby right out her va-jay-jay."

Tippi giggled.

Pippa shook her head, and I breathed a sigh of relief when she smiled. "I'm ready to pop this kid out. I say, show me the cobra!" She said the last bit Jerry Maguire-style.

"It'll happen soon enough," Gilly said. "Then you'll be begging to stick 'em back in."

Pippa laughed. "I can guarantee that won't happen. Unless raising them turns me gray..." she let the word linger, then giggled as Gilly whacked her shoulder.

"You wait and see. Once they're out, you are no longer in control of their every moment. It's scary."

"Like snakes," Pippa said.

"Worse," said Gilly.

We all laughed.

"Is that guy going to live?" Tippi asked.

"I don't know. He was in bad shape when the ambulance took off with him." I snapped my fingers excitedly. "Oh, Gilly. You will never believe who I ran into."

"Who?"

"Perry Porter."

"You're kidding me. Is he fat and bald?"

"Nope," I said. "He's still pretty cute. He's a conservation officer now."

"Really?" she asked wistfully. "I had the biggest lady boner for him back in high school."

"I told him," I said.

Gilly pulled her shoulders back. "You didn't."

I shook my head. "I'm kidding. I didn't even bring you up."

She put her elbows on the counter and rested her chin in her palm. "What a pal."

I made a kissy face. "You love me."

"Lord help me, I do," Gilly said.

Tippi slid Marjorie Meadow's flyer in front of us. "Are we going to the creepy doll show on Friday?"

I made eye contact with Pippa. "Oh, will you still be here on Friday?"

"Tippi's going to be staying for a couple of weeks," Pippa said.

"How nice," I replied, unsure if it was a good thing or not. I wondered if Tippi's timing, with Pippa at the end of her third trimester, couldn't have been better. Even so, I would support Pippa however she wanted. "Ezra and I are planning on going. We should go as a group."

"I'd like that," Gilly said.

"Do you want to come over before for a barbeque? Business has been slow in the store, and Jordy has been aching for a reason to slow smoke brisket overnight." She gave her belly a pat. "Besides, Baby Davenport-Hines loves spicy barbeque sauce."

"I'm in," I said. "I'll come over early and help you get stuff ready."

"Me too," Gilly said. "It'll be fun."

Pippa cast us grateful looks. "Great. You can bring dates if you want."

"I'll ask Ezra."

"My date doesn't live around here," Gilly pouted.

"Do you want me to ask Perry for you?"

"I'm going to smack you hard," Gilly threatened. "Maybe I'll ask Scott."

"Good idea." I sighed at our empty store. "Why don't we close up shop early today? I think we can all use an afternoon off."

"The electrician for the doorbell did cancel for today. He said he can't get out here until Saturday now," Pippa said. "Okay. I vote for closing early."

"Me too," Gilly seconded.

"Hey, there's that cute paramedic," Tippi said as she pointed to the windows. Outside, Handsome Grant was strolling past the shop.

"I wonder if he's been to see Carrie today. I still need to do that." I hurried to the door and pushed it open. "Grant!" I called after him.

He stopped and looked back at me. "Oh, hey," he called back. He did not walk toward me, so I was forced to go to him. Even then, he didn't face me. He was too busy waiting for the walk light to turn green. "Can I help you with something? You didn't find any more snakes, did you?"

I wasn't looking for a long conversation, so I skipped telling him about the king cobra incident. "I wondered if you checked in on Carrie today. How's she doing?"

"I was at the hospital this morning. She seems to be better." He scratched his head, and I noticed a faded tattoo in the shape of a spade, like a suit on playing cards, behind his ear at the hairline. The doctors say if the swelling keeps going down, they'll transfer her out of the ICU tomorrow."

"That's great news."

"Sure is." The light turned green. He gave me a two-finger wave goodbye, which I guess was better than the one-finger alternative. "See you around."

CHAPTER 14

I texted Ezra to meet me at Moo-La-Lattes when he got through at the snake farm. Pippa and Tippi came with me to the coffee shop, but Gilly wanted to be home when Marco got there so she could talk to him some more about fighting and the recent slip in his grades. Personally, I thought Marco had Senioritis, an affliction Gilly and I knew all about as seniors in high school, but I wasn't his mother. Gilly often saw things when it came to Ari and Marco long before I did.

Davis Meadows was at the crappy table again, laptop open and thoroughly engrossed. Tippi grabbed the first table near the doors while Pippa waddled over to the bar and leaned in so Jordy could kiss her. I saw her wince as she straightened. If she was in pain, I wished she'd tell me. I'd tried to convince her to cut her hours at the shop until after her maternity leave, but she wouldn't hear of it.

"Mothers used to work in fields until it was time to

squat down and squeeze a kid out. I think I can handle a few hours a day behind a cash register," she'd said.

I had reminded her that those mothers didn't have a Nora Black in their corners.

Jordy waved at me. "The usual?"

"You know it." I looped my arm in Pippa's. "You go sit and put your feet up. I'll bring over the drinks."

Jordy shook his head. "I'll bring them over, and neither of you has to wait." He winked at Pippa. "Perks of sleeping with the owner."

She smiled, and her whole face lit up. While Pippa went to the table Tippi had grabbed, I walked over to Davis. He wasn't even aware of me as his finger danced across the mousepad.

I tapped the table. "Are you renting space here?"

Davis looked up at me and blinked as if he didn't recognize me at first. Then he shook his head. "Nora. Hi. I didn't see you come in." He nodded toward Jordy. "And you're right, I should pay Jordy. We have no Wi-Fi in the gallery right now, and I don't want to go home to work on the website."

"Wi-Fi is free to all my customers," Jordy said to Davis. "As long as you're drinking coffee," he amended, "you can sit there as long as you want."

Davis held up his empty cup. "I'll take another one."

I couldn't help myself. I peeked at his screen. He was on the ArtsyAuction website and watching the bidding for a sunflower painting that had the description *718 14 Yellow Sunflowers along 9 French pavement stones, 3.3 total weight for shipping.* The seller was someone named O.R. Diamant, and the bid was at two thousand dollars.

"That's an expensive sunflower," I said. "Is the artist someone famous?" The picture was pretty, but it lacked any real intensity. I'd seen better art hanging on the wall of a hotel room.

Davis closed his laptop. "I don't know the artist," he said. "I'm trying to get more familiar with how these auctions are run so I can add some of the gallery's pieces."

"That makes sense." His eyes darted toward the door. I looked over. No one had come in. Oh. He wanted to make an escape. From me? Why? "I'll let you get back to work."

He gave me a tight smile before looking at his watch then standing up. "I need to get back to the gallery, anyhow. Can I get the coffee to-go, Jordy?"

Jordy dumped the frothy drink into a takeaway cup. He put a lid and a sleeve on it. "Here you go, Davis." Davis put his laptop in his satchel, slung it over his shoulder, grabbed his coffee, then set a ten-dollar bill on the counter. "Keep the change."

"Have a nice day," Jordy said as he dropped the money into his cash register, taking two dollars and a few coins from the till to place in the tip jar.

I grabbed Davis' empty cup and saucer for the table and took it to Jordy. "Sorry. Wasn't trying to run off your customers."

"I'm not worried about Davis." He took the dishes

from me and glanced at Pippa and Tippi, who were having an intense conversation.

"Are you worried about them?"

He shook his head. "Nah, they'll work it out." He shrugged. "Or they won't."

I was rooting for the Davenport women. I hoped Pippa and Tippi could find common ground. "Pippa told me that Tippi has a history of partying and getting into trouble. But everything I've seen this past couple of days, it seems like Tippi is trying to…you know, walk the straight and narrow."

Jordy began preparing our drinks. "Here's the thing, though, when you're in recovery, you can be as sorry for past mistakes as you want, but it doesn't mean the people you've wronged have to forgive you."

"Tippi is in recovery?"

Jordy paused. "I didn't say that."

But he'd inferred it. Was Tippi attending meetings? And if so, did Pippa know? I decided to change the subject.

"I bet your family is proud of you," I said. "You've made such a good life for yourself. I bet they're excited about the baby, too."

Jordy smiled, but I saw misery in his expression. "I haven't talked to my parents in fourteen years. Not since the day I showed up on their porch, and they told me that they never wanted to see me again. That I no longer had a home."

"That's awful, Jordy." I couldn't imagine my parents ever telling me something like that. "It's beyond harsh."

He smiled and gave a slight head shake. "Harsh is me pawning my mother's crystal birds she'd inherited from her grandmother so I could buy drugs. Harsh is me showing up at my sister's wedding so high that I fell into the wedding cake and vomited on the dance floor." His tone grew more pained. "Harsh is getting my cousin Mike high for the first time when he was barely eighteen." These were old wounds, but I could tell he still felt each of them with deep regret. "All those moments and dozens more that I put my family through, that's harsh. Them telling me they never wanted to see me again?" His gaze grew distant as he relived the moment in a memory. "That was survival. Their survival. You see, they'd given me a second chance before, and a third, and a fourth. Would I have liked a fifth chance? Of course. Did they owe it to me? Absolutely not. I can't blame them. I'd proven over and over that I was a junkie who would do anything to get another fix, including lying about my sobriety."

"But you've been sober for over a decade. You sponsor people. You have this great business and the best woman who loves you with all her might."

His blue eyes softened at the corners. "I'm lucky," he said. "But I'm still an addict. And the only thing between present-day me and past me is one bad decision."

Damn. His words were like a punch to the gut.

"Anyways," he said, forcing his tone lighter. "Tippi can ask for forgiveness for her transgressions against Pippa, but ultimately, Pippa doesn't have to forgive her. But if the woman wants to change," he looked over at his soon-to-be sister-in-law, "and I think she does, then she has to start with forgiving herself. It's the only way to make the change stick."

My vision blurred with tears. "That's good advice for everyone." I thought about Dolly and her twenty-year sobriety chip and the empty vodka bottle in her purse. "Did Dolly Paris ever come to any of your meetings?"

"Pippa told me you'd be asking about Dolly."

"I think she'd been sober for a long time," I said. "What would make her fall off the wagon?"

"A Tuesday," he said. "Addicts don't need a reason to use, Nora. Every day, you have to find reasons to stay sober. As long as you have those, you have a fighting chance."

"You are really good at this," I said.

"At what?" he asked.

"Talking to people. I can see why Pippa loves you so much."

Pippa came up behind me, catching the last part of what I'd said. She put her arms over my shoulders. "The fact that he's got a nice butt doesn't hurt, either," she said.

I thought about Ezra and giggled. "It certainly doesn't."

Jordy dug around behind the counter, then produced a card and handed it to me. It said, "White Rose Church, Tuesdays (C), Wednesdays (O), and Sundays (C), 7:00 p.m."

"What's this?" I asked.

"That's the weekly AA meetings in town. The group I hold is NA, narcotics anonymous. I get alcoholics who come to mine, but they all had drug addictions as well. If Dolly attended meetings here in town, it would be there."

"And they meet every Tuesday?" Maybe I could go this evening and see if anyone knew anything about Dolly.

"Yep, but Tuesday meetings are closed. So are the Sunday ones, meaning only members of the group can attend. Those are the nights where we can get brutally honest about our pasts. But see, the O next to Wednesday? That's an open meeting for people interested in getting sober and non-alcoholics who want to observe. If you're going to go," he said, smiling, "and I know you are. Tomorrow night is your night."

"Do you know anyone from that group?"

"I attended meetings there when I first moved to Garden Cove." He wagged a finger at me. "And before you ask, no, I don't remember Dolly at any of those meetings, but frankly, I was too busy taking care of myself back then to pay attention to other people."

I tucked the card into my purse. "Got it. I really appreciate the information."

"No problem." He shrugged. "My advice? Find Dolly's sponsor if she had one. It will most likely be a woman, but that's not always the case."

"Thank you."

Jordy met my gaze. "With your nose-for-news gift and their baggage, you might see more than you bargain for."

"It's possible," I admitted.

His expression became more serious. "I need you to

promise me that as long as the information you discover has nothing to do with Dolly Paris, you keep it to yourself. There's a reason these meetings are anonymous."

I hadn't thought about all the secrets I might encounter that had nothing to do with the case. "I promise," I told him. "If it doesn't have any bearing on Dolly, I won't share anything I accidentally sniff out."

CHAPTER 15

The five o'clock news blared on the television in Carrie's ICU room. Her coloring was less pale than the day before, and her fingers on her left hand were less bratwursts and more breakfast sausages in appearance.

I knocked on the door frame to alert her to my presence. She smiled wanly in my direction before turning the television off with a button on her call light control.

She gestured toward the TV with a nod. "Weatherman's calling for snow again next week."

I nodded. "That's what they're saying. This past week has given me a taste for spring. I'm not ready for it to turn cold again."

"Come on in," she said. There were several bouquets of flowers and a few stuffed bears with get-well balloons on the ledge of her window.

"Have you been getting many visitors today?" I asked.

"A few. Everyone expressing their sympathy about mom." Her tone was slightly bitter. "Hypocrites."

"What do you mean?"

"People like Dana Rigby, Marjorie Meadows, and Tanya Jones. Those ladies made Mom feel isolated and alone. And, now that she's dead, they want to act like they cared about her." She shook her head and winced in pain as she rotated away from the wall of sympathy. "I'm sick of them, and I'm sick of Garden Cove."

I knew what it was like to have people who had stopped seeing mom during the last year of her illness come out in droves to express how much they would miss her after she was gone. They certainly hadn't missed her while she was alive, and I'll admit, I'd felt a little bit of resentment. Ultimately, I knew my anger had resulted from my grief, though, not a lot to do with the fair-weather mourners.

"You don't have to keep the flowers. I'll ask the nurse to take them out of the room for you, if you want," I offered. "Or I'll do it."

Her eyes watered up again. "No, I don't want that." Her gaze shifted to meet mine. "I know Mom had her problems. Believe me, I know."

"Most people have problems," I said. "No one's perfect, and if they say they are, they're lying."

Carrie gave me a fleeting smile. "Thanks for that." She shook her head. "But Mom had her demons. More than most."

"The drinking," I said.

Her expression turned stark as she drew her covers up with her good hand. "You knew?"

"Only suspected, and only because I found a bottle of alcohol in her purse when I was searching for your insurance card Sunday."

"Mom was good at hiding it," she said. "When I was little, she would go on binges. God, that woman could drink herself into a stupor for a week. But then she'd be fine. Sober as a judge for a couple of months, then she'd go on another bender."

"I'm so sorry." I remembered the little girl cooking cinnamon toast for her inebriated mother. I couldn't imagine how scary it must have been for someone so young to feel like she had to take care of the adult in her life. "But she got sober, right? I found AA coins at her house."

"For a long time," Carrie said. "But the last few months, I'd started worrying she'd started up again." Her lower lip began to quiver. "I shouldn't have moved out. This wouldn't have happened if I'd stayed at home."

"Her drinking or her death?" I asked gently.

"Both, I suppose."

"You can't control anyone's actions but your own," I said. "And diseases don't give a damn about people."

Carrie shook her head. "Your mom died of cancer. She didn't have a blood alcohol level of point-two-four in her system when she passed away." Her lips thinned into a grim line. "Reese came by today and asked me about her drinking because of Mom's blood alcohol level when she died. People will find a way to blame Mom. I know they will." Her tears streamed fresh on her cheeks.

I dragged a few tissues from the box on her bedside table and handed them to her. "You shouldn't worry about things like that, honey. People will say what they are going to say, but in my experience, no one likes to speak ill of someone who has passed. You'll hear many great stories about your mom. Tales that you didn't even know existed and those are the narratives you need to hold on to. They are the ones that will get you by in your darkest minutes."

"You think so?"

I nodded. "I heard many tales of my mother's life after she died that, as her child, I never knew. Most of the time, parents let us love them with blinders on." I chuck-led. It was something Gilly had said to me when I'd found out my mom had dated several men over the years after my father died, including Michael Drummer, a guy who owned a riverboat that gave tours on the lake. "I mean, parents often try to show us who they want us to see, not who they actually are. But children," I took Carrie's hand, "we're not much better, are we? We don't show all of ourselves to our parents either, because we don't want to disappoint them."

"Or worse," Carrie said, "show them that their worst fears about us have come true."

Marjorie had said that Carrie and her mom had been fighting about a guy Carrie was dating who reminded Dolly of the past. "Is that something you're worried about?"

"Maybe." She shook her head. "I don't know. Mom was always so paranoid about men. But if you're someone who's always shouting it's gonna rain, you're bound to be right at least a few times."

Honestly, until Gilly had told me about Dolly's past on Monday, or what little she knew, I'd never thought about who Carrie's father was or where he might be. "Is this about your dad?"

Carrie shrugged. "Yes and no."

"Do you know him?"

"He died in October," she said. "But no, I didn't know him. I'd never even met him. I was contacted by a man at the Department of Corrections that he'd died, and he asked if I wanted to come collect his belongings?"

My mouth dropped open, and I snapped it shut. I don't know what I'd expected to learn but finding out that Carrie's father had died in prison had not been on any list. "You never knew about him?"

"No, but he knew all about me. When I received the package of his stuff, he had pictures of me at different times in my life. Here, I'd always thought my bio dad was a one-night stand my mom had taken home when she was drunk, but instead, he was someone who had known about me, who Mom kept up on my life, but I was never allowed to know about him."

"Is that why you moved out?"

"Yes," she said. "I was angry with mom for a while, but I forgave her, Nora. You have to believe me."

"When your mom was struggling with her asthma, I saw the way you jumped right up to help her. You loved her, and she knew it. That's what you hold on to." Carrie had to be in her late twenties now, which meant her father had probably been a lifer. "Do you know why he had been in prison?"

Carrie swallowed hard then nodded. "Felony murder." She gripped my hand tightly. "You won't tell anyone, will you? I don't know if I could handle it right now."

Felony murder was when someone died during a felony, planned or unplanned. Even if the person was killed by someone other than the perpetrator, it's *still* felony murder. My vision at Dolly's house, the woman had said there weren't supposed to be guns. That someone had died because of the man. She'd been blonde, but Dolly could have dyed her hair that color at some point.

The past should stay in the past. Had Dolly been worried the past was catching up to her? I couldn't promise Carrie to keep this information a secret, especially if it had something to do with Dolly's death. "You know I see Ezra Holden, right?"

"Yes."

"I am going to tell him about your father, but only because it might shed some light on your mom's case. I promise you that he'll keep it quiet. No one needs to find out if the information leads nowhere. Will you tell me his name?"

Carrie sighed, but the tension around her eyes had eased as if she'd been waiting to unburden her fears to someone. "David Summers."

"Thank you for trusting me."

She sniffled. "Mom always liked you, you know. She said you were genuine." She loosened her grip. "I think she was right."

The compliment caught me off guard, and I felt the pinch of guilt. I'd always considered Dolly more a friendly acquaintance than a close friend, but I had liked her. "Maybe if I'd been more genuine, I would have seen she was in trouble." I let go of her hand. "If you need anything, you call me, okay?"

CHAPTER 16

I'd put on my comfiest pajamas, popped some popcorn, and poured myself a glass of Diet Coke. I sipped and nibbled as I lounged on my couch, feet up on the armrest while I prepared to search for David Summers on my laptop. I'd called Ezra and told him about my conversation with Carrie and the revelation of her father's identity.

How had meek and mild Dolly kept such a colorful past secret? Especially in a small community like Garden Cove?

I typed in David Summers, Felony Murder. The number of people named David Summers or David or Summer was in the dozens. I skipped recent cases, cases where the defendant was over fifty, and cases out of state. There was a sparse article from 1992 that looked promising. Still, it turned out to be for a Davina Summers, and it was first-degree murder, not felony murder.

Before I knew it, an hour had passed by. It was amazing how time flew by when you went down rabbit holes on the internet. Since Ezra, who had access to actual law enforcement resources, had promised to call me if he found anything out, I stopped searching for David Summers.

On a whim, I typed in ArtsyAuctions. I still couldn't believe someone had been willing to pay thousands of dollars for a remedial painting of sunflowers. I mean, it wasn't as if the painting had been a Picasso.

In the search bar, I put in O.R. Diamante, and forty auctions came up. It was a mix of paintings, sculptures, and photographs. I couldn't see any theme between the pieces, and they were all decent, but to my untrained eye, they seemed pedestrian.

A knock at the door startled me. Ezra had Mason staying the night with him, so I hadn't been expecting company. "Just a minute," I yelled, looking for a robe.

"It's me, Aunt Nora," Ari yelled. "You don't have to put on a bra on my account."

I snorted a giggle as I unlocked the front door and let her in. "What's going on?" Usually, Ari stayed tucked into her studies on school nights. She was one of two girls in her school who were in the STEM accelerated program. A program that integrated science, technology, engineering, and math. In other words, the girl was a smart as a whip.

"I can't take the drama between Mom and Marco tonight. I have an exam this Friday for my AP STEM math class, and if I don't get some peace and quiet, I'm going to fail."

"You've never failed a thing in your life," I said as she walked in, her backpack over her shoulder. I closed the door behind her. "Have you eaten?"

"Yes," she said. "I don't need food, just a place to study."

"That's probably good since all I could offer you is popcorn, breath mints, and toast. I haven't gotten to the grocery store in a couple of weeks."

She sat down on the couch and peered at my open laptop. "Are you buying art?" She picked up the computer and put it on her knees. "This stuff looks like the poster art you can buy at Everything-Mart." Her eyes widened. "Wow, some of this stuff is going for a lot of money. Maybe I'm studying the wrong thing. I should take liberal arts. I'm pretty sure I could've taken that photograph of the old Chevy."

"You will not be quitting your dreams to pursue art, young lady," I said. "I mean unless you really want to." I sat down next to her as she clicked on the truck photo.

The bid was at forty-seven hundred dollars. "Are you kidding me? I'm beginning to think *I'm* in the wrong business."

"And it still has three days left on the auction." Ari shook her head. "This description makes no sense to me at all," she said. "Go Platinum. A Cushioned Ride. One headlight. Two-point-five shipping weight."

"You mean two and a half pounds?"

"No. There's no unit of measurement." I looked where she pointed.

Sure enough, it said, *2.5 shipping weight.*

"Don't bid on it, Aunt Nora. I'll take a picture of an old truck for you and won't charge anything but what it costs to enlarge it for a frame."

"I have no plans to buy it." I clicked on the next auction. It was a quartz sculpture of a duck, with the description *011 Little Ducks All In A Row. 3.9 total shipping weight,* and it was going for over four thousand in bids so far. "This is crazy." I could see why Davis was excited to get some of the gallery work onto the auction site. A few sales like these could really keep Marjorie afloat. "Okay, kiddo. I'm not taking you down this rabbit hole with me and be the reason you do poorly on your exam. You can have my office or the spare room. Take your pick."

Ari gave me a look of pure gratitude. She raspberried my cheek and laughed at the face I made. "Thanks, Aunt Nora. You're the best."

"That's what I hear."

* * *

MY RINGING PHONE woke me up. I'd fallen asleep on the couch while watching *Bridget Jones Diary*, the first one, for the umpteenth time. The last thing I remembered before drifting off was Colin Firth wearing an ugly Christmas sweater.

Ezra's name was on the call display, and it was 5:00

a.m. in the morning. Gah, I'd slept all night on the couch. I rubbed the sleep from my eyes and answered the call.

"Morning," I said. My throat was dry and scratchy. "It's a bit early for a wake-up call."

"Johnny Scales didn't make it." His voice was soft and easy, just like his nickname.

The news got my attention. I sat up straight. "Well, that sucks. Did he ever come around enough to answer any questions?"

"Unfortunately, he didn't." Ezra sounded tired. "We didn't find anything at his farm to point us in the right direction either."

"It was a stretch to think he'd keep receipts, but you never know."

"Nope," he agreed. "I feel like we can't catch a freaking break on this case."

"Have you been to sleep yet?" I asked.

"Not yet," he admitted. "I do have some news on David Summers, though."

"Well, don't bury the lead."

He chuckled, and I felt giddy as I walked down the hall to the bathroom. The Diet Coke from the previous night was stretching my bladder. "And hurry up unless you want to listen to me pee."

"I've heard you pee before. My cabin has thin walls."

"Shut up," I said with a laugh. "Hurry up and spill before I do."

"He was part of a heist crew that had knocked over several jewelry stores, small banks, and check cashing facilities around the state. One of the robberies ended up with one of the crew members dead. Shot by a security guard and at a Check Plus. The store had only recently hired armed security, so the crew had been taken by surprise. Two got away."

Obviously, I was not getting off this phone anytime soon, and I really had to go. "I'm putting you on mute," I said. "Keep talking, though. I can hear you."

"A guy named Roger Tracy was the thief who was killed," Ezra continued. "David Summers was caught two months later trying to knock over a pawn shop on his own. The third member of the crew was never caught. He just disappeared. David was charged with Felony Murder. And, because he wouldn't give up the money they'd stolen or the third robber, he was given a max sentence of life without parole."

I finished peeing and washed my hands before unmuting him. "Wow. That's loyalty. How much money did they get away with?"

"Twenty jobs over six months. They'd accumulated a tidy sum of over eight hundred thousand dollars in cash and jewelry."

I went into the kitchen, put the phone on speaker, and set it on the counter. "That's a tidy sum all right." I turned on my drip coffee maker. I desperately needed coffee and a shower.

"I have a proposition for you," Ezra said.

"It's wicked early in the morning, and I am not caffeinated yet, but I could probably manage some phone sex."

Ezra snorted. "Hold that thought because I like where

you're going with it, but that wasn't the proposition I had in mind. I talked to Chief Rafferty, and he's agreed to let you go through Dolly's Dollhouse Emporium and her house again for any psychic vibes you might get. I think Johnny Scales' death by snake and the fact that we aren't getting anywhere has him rattled."

"Hah, rattled, like a rattler," I said. "Clever. But, yes, as a good citizen, I will gladly put my nose to work for the Garden Cove Police Department."

"Great. How about I meet you in town at six-thirty?"

"You mean an hour and a half from now? Don't you need to sleep?"

"I'll get in a forty-minute cat nap right now," he said. "Unless you can think of better ways to spend that time…"

"Why, Ezra Holden, I would love to get creative with you over the phone, but I don't want you falling asleep as we get started."

"No fear in that happening, sweetheart."

Ari strolled into the kitchen, still wearing her clothes from the night before. I hadn't realized she was still here.

"You two need to get a room," she said.

"This whole house is my room," I countered.

She smiled, then leaned to the phone. "Good morning, Detective Easy."

"Morning, Ari," he said with humor and warmth.

I picked up the phone and took it off speaker. "Let's meet at seven. That'll give you a few more minutes to rest."

"Sounds good, sweetheart. Love you."

"Love you back," I replied.

When I set the phone back down, Ari was already pouring herself a cup of coffee. She took a sip and sighed with satisfaction.

"Is my coffee good?"

"It's the only food you excel at," Ari remarked. She smiled. "I'm glad you're happy, Aunt Nora."

"Thanks, Ari." I walked over and gave the girl a hug. "Me too."

CHAPTER 17

The temperature was down in the twenties this morning, so I wore my heavier winter coat. It was a dark lavender peplum puffer coat that flared at the waist and gave me a faux hourglass waistline. I'd bought complementary lavender-gray mittens, along with fuzzy boots and a hat to go with it. Not going to lie. The look was adorable. And honestly, it was the only reason I'd looked forward to any cold weather this winter.

Ezra and Reese waited outside the front door of Dolly's Dollhouse Emporium and Museum. I was ten minutes early, which meant he didn't take my advice on the longer nap. The museum was in one of the few brick-and-mortar, turn-of-the-century buildings. When Garden Cove was first founded, the place had been a Five & Dime general store. Granted, that was way before my time, but my father had remembered the store fondly every time he drove past it.

After the Five & Dime closed, it had become a pharmacy and stayed one until I left for college. Dolly had purchased the place to make her doll museum. You wouldn't think a place that did antique doll tours would be a moneymaker, but she had made the business successful.

I parked in front of the building. Reese waved as I got out of the car. "Damn, it's bitter cold out this morning. I was just starting to get used to the warmer weather." Her gaze ran appraisingly over my attire. "I want that coat," she said. "And those boots." She threw up her hands. "Screw it. I want the mittens and the hat, too."

I'm not going to say I preened and pranced my way over to them like a show pony, but I might have shown off a little. "I'm fancy," I told her.

"Hah!" she laughed. "You sure are."

"Morning, Ezra." I turned and flipped my peplum.

He took my hand and twirled me around and dipped me back for a smooch that was more a greeting than an invitation. He wiggled his eyebrows. "Winter looks good on you."

Reese cleared her throat. "Official police business going on here." She jangled a set of keys.

Ezra set me upright. He straightened his coat. "Let's get to officiating."

Reese unlocked the door. "How do you want to do this, Nora? Should we wait outside?"

"That might be better, in case any of the scents in there trigger a walk down memory lane for one of you. I mean, do you really want me to see any doll-related trauma you might have experienced in the past?"

Reese wrinkled her nose. "Good call."

Ezra held the door open for me. "Holler if you see something."

I smiled. "If I scent something, I'll say something."

"Hardy-har, Nancy Shrew," Reese replied.

I chuckled. "Did you just come up with that, or have you been holding onto it for just such an occasion?"

"I've been holding onto it for a while now," she admitted. "It's not quite on the nose, though." She smirked.

"Keep trying. You'll get there." I took off my mittens and tucked them away in my coat pockets, then opened my purse and took out a pair of latex gloves.

Ezra's eyes widened. "You've come prepared."

"We can play doctor later." I snapped a fingertip on my right hand. "Anyhow, there might be evidence or rat droppings in there." I took one cleansing, calming breath and walked into the doll museum.

Porcelain and ceramic dolls lined shelves. Some of the more fragile and expensive were displayed behind glass, along with several styles of dollhouses, doll clothing displays, costume jewelry, and accessories. Since moving back to Garden Cove, I'd been inside once when all the business owners took the resort tour for fun. Dolly's was the first stop. When Dolly had shown us around, her enthusiasm for the history of dolls and doll making had given the place a feeling of warmth, vibrancy, and history. Now, the interior felt cold and gray, and not just because of the weather. It was as if the place had lost its soul.

The maze of aisles in the museum was designed to

take customers on a walk-through history. The displays started with modern-day dolls made with laser precision and went all the way back to figures of the mid-1800s. While Dolly had kept the place spotless, there was still a scent of mustiness similar to that of a damp book.

Unfortunately, I was getting a lot of random remembrances of small children playing tea parties and other such games that come with having dolls, but nothing that specifically pointed to Dolly or a motive for her death. I rounded a corner near her desk and a display of books on the history of dolls. The sharp tang of lemon and pine made me sneeze.

"What do you want?" a woman asks. I recognize her voice and her pearl button cardigan. It's Dolly, and she's straightening the books on the rack. She's wearing an apron around her waist, its pockets bulging with what I assume is cleaning supplies.

"I know what you're hiding, Dolly. You can pay me, or I can go to the cops with your little secret," a man says. His voice is low and hushed as he stands in the shadows. Most of the lights are out except for blinking, colorful fairy lights that highlight the display along with frosted garland.

"If you tell the police, I might go to jail, but so will you. Blackmail is illegal, too."

"I'm just a good citizen doing my duty," he says blandly. "That's all they'll hear when I make my report."

"Get out," Dolly seethes. "I know your type. You won't do crap that doesn't somehow benefit you."

"Okay, then. I'll just tell your sweetheart of a daughter

about your misspent youth. I'm sure she would love to know what trash her mother used to be."

"Leave Carrie out of this."

He moves from the shadows, his voice quiet and menacing. "I will, if you give me what I want."

"I don't have them here," she says.

"You have until the end of the week." He leaves.

Even though I can't see her face, I know she's crying from the way her chest heaves. She reaches around the backside of the book rack and retrieves a bottle clearly marked gin. She unscrews the top, the liquid sloshes out of the opening as she lifts it up to drink. After, she pulls a cleaning rag from her pockets and wipes the spill away.

When the scent-memory ended, I looked at the display. There were no lights or garland around the rack now, so I had to presume the vision took place near Christmas time. Cripes, had someone been black-mailing Dolly for the past two months? The fear in her voice after he'd threatened to tell Carrie had been thick and palpable. Why had she been so confident he wouldn't go to the police, and yet, just as sure he'd tell her daughter whatever awful thing she'd wanted to hide?

On a whim, I reached behind the display, unsurprised when I found a bottle. I gripped the neck and took it from its hiding place. Only, this wasn't the small pint of gin Dolly had been drinking in the memory. This was a fifth of premium vodka, and the bottle was almost empty. I unscrewed the cap and took a whiff.

"We did it, baby!" the young blonde woman jumps up onto

a tall man wrapping her legs around his waist. "I can't believe we did it!"

He has a bottle in his hand and takes a drink. Eagerly, she takes it from him and takes her own long, slow pull.

"I'm going to marry you," he says. "When this is all over, and we're set for life. I'm going to give you the life you dream of. A house. White picket fences. Babies. The works."

"I've been waiting for you my whole life, Dodger," she says.

"I've been right here, Dolls," he tells her. "Right here waiting for you."

The woman takes her top off as the man carries her down the hall.

I blinked the vision away. *Right here waiting for you.* The gold band in her small treasure chest, the one that she had kept the lock of hair with the key and the AA medallions in, it had been inscribed with the words *Right Here Waiting.*

I felt unsteady and out of sorts after the last aroma-mojo hit. By the time I got to the front door, I was stumbling. My knees buckled as I stepped out onto the sidewalk.

"Nora," Ezra said. He put his arm around me. "You look pale."

"And sweaty," Reese said. "You look like you just ran a marathon."

I handed Ezra the vodka bottle then unzipped my coat to let the cold wash over my overheated body. "I found this behind a book rack."

"You need to sit down." He looked anxious, and I wondered just how bad I looked.

"I'm okay," I assured him. The wintery wind had done the job of clearing my mind and restoring my strength. The last vision, the one of Dolly and her lover, had been potent. The stronger the emotions were behind the memories I saw, the harder they were to recover from.

"What did you see?" he asked.

"Dolly was being blackmailed."

"For what?" Reese asked.

"I'm not sure, but it was something she didn't want Carrie to find out about. It was the only thing the blackmailer said to her that made her afraid." I thought back to their conversation. "She wasn't afraid of him," I said. "I mean, not physically. That's strange."

"Unless he was someone she knew well," Reese said.

"She definitely knew the guy." I nodded.

"Do you think it was someone she was seeing?" Ezra asked.

I took the latex gloves off. Ezra handed me my purse, and I dropped them inside. "Seeing as in dating?"

"Or just sleeping with," Reese mused.

I zipped my coat back up. "It didn't feel as if they were intimate, but that doesn't mean they weren't or that they hadn't been in the past. Oh, and she had Christmas decorations up."

"So, this could have happened as far back as November."

Reese shook her head. "Dolly was the kind of woman who would have waited until after Thanksgiving to put up Christmas. We can ask Carrie if she knows when her mom would have decorated for the holiday."

"And when she usually took them down. It could give us sort of a timeline since there are no decorations in there now," I added. "Of course, there is nothing to say that the blackmail started recently. What I saw could have taken place years ago." The twenty-something-degree weather was seeping into my bones now. I rubbed my fingers together to warm them.

Ezra plucked my mittens from my pockets and put them on me. The frown on his face told me he was still worried. I smiled at him. "I'm fine, I promise."

"Did you see anything else?" he asked.

"Yes, when I smelled the vodka, I got another memory of the young blonde woman that I'd seen when I found Dolly. Only this time, she wasn't fighting with the man. They were celebrating."

"What?"

"Some victory." I shrugged. "She called the man Dodger, and..." I remembered the way she'd laughed when he'd carried her down the hall. *I've been here, Dolls. Right here waiting for you.* "And I think he loved her very much."

CHAPTER 18

I left my car in town and rode with Ezra out to Dolly's lake house. He twisted his hands on the steering wheel, his jaw clenched tight as he watched the road ahead.

I closed my eyes and rested my forehead against the icy passenger window. I opened them when I felt his hand on my thigh. I slipped my fingers through his, and he pulled my hand up and kissed my knuckle.

"We don't have to do this now," he said. "Or at all."

"I know, but I want to, Ezra. I would tell you if I didn't." I sat up straight and looked at him. "What's going on with you? You're usually not this…overprotective."

He was silent for a long moment before he said, "You didn't see the way you looked when you came out of there. You looked…you looked like someone who was dying."

I unbuckled my seatbelt and skootched across the seat until I could put my head on his shoulder. "I'm sorry I scared you. I promise you, I'm not dying. At least not any faster than anyone else."

He gave me a quick kiss on the forehead while keeping his gaze on the road. "I love you, Nora. All of you. Your stubbornness, your independence, your humor, your intelligence, and your beauty…"

"Stop," I said. Then jokingly added, "but do go on."

He chuckled. "I'm just saying, you are everything I want in a woman."

"But…"

"No buts. The thing is, I know if I hold you too tightly that I'll suffocate all the things about you that I love. I don't want to do that, but sometimes it's hard to reconcile that with the part of my brain that wants to keep you safe."

"It's killing you that I don't have my seatbelt on, isn't it?"

His smile turned into a bemused grin. "It really is."

I slid back over to my side of the cab and belted myself back in. "See," I told him. "I'm not unreasonable."

"Not at all," he agreed. He tapped the blinker lever as he slowed the truck. "We're here."

Reese had beat us to Dolly's. She was on the porch, bouncing around to stay warm. "Took you guys long enough. I feel like I've been here for ages."

She only left a few minutes before us, so we hadn't been that far behind. "I know an exaggeration when I hear it," I told her. "Besides, you could've waited in the car."

The wind blew Reese's strawberry blonde hair into

her face. She brushed it back. "I could have, but then I wouldn't have had any reason to complain." She gestured at the door. "It's unlocked. Do you want us to go in with you this time or no?"

It made me feel good that she offered me the choice instead of trying to make the decision for me. "You guys can come in."

I swear I saw the worry lines in Ezra's forehead vanish like magic. "If that's what you want," he said nonchalantly.

I arched a brow as I walked past him and went inside the A-frame home.

"Okay," Reese said. "Dolly's house has a simple layout. Obviously, living room upfront. Just up ahead, the area is split in two, with a kitchen on the right and the bathroom on the left. You guys found Dolly in the space between. There is a narrow path between the two rooms that open to a hall with a utility room on the left and a home office on the right. On the left in front of the utility room is a staircase that leads to a large master bed and bath that takes up the entire loft."

"This is a beautiful place," I said.

"The loft bedroom has a balcony that overlooks the lake. Prime realty." Reese gave a low whistle. "If Carrie decides to sell this place, I think she can get a small fortune for it."

"That's a motive," I said.

"I didn't mean—" She squinted at me. "Damn. That is a motive."

"I don't think Carrie had anything to do with her mom's death, though."

"We can't rule anything out at this point," Ezra said. "I hope Carrie didn't have anything to do with her mother's death, but you never know."

"She has an excellent alibi."

"Sometimes criminals hire other criminals to do the dirty work," he said.

I sighed. "True enough." But in my gut, I knew Carrie's grief for her mother had been real. She was a daughter torn up by the loss. "I still don't think she's guilty."

"She's not a serious suspect," Ezra admitted. "But that's where we're at. We have a bunch of nothing to go on, which is why it wasn't too hard to convince Chief Rafferty to let you have a stab at it. The mayor is on his butt for results." He gave me an open palm shrug. "Desperate times, and all."

I guess I was desperate measures. I took a couple of deep breaths to calm my brain, then nodded. "I'm ready to take my stab."

It struck me how nothing much had changed since Monday morning when Gilly and I had found Dolly on the floor near her kitchen, except for the no dead body part, of course. But otherwise, the police had been respectful when they'd searched the place. I walked down the hall, reliving my own memories of that day. The living room was a good twenty-four feet wide, but the depth was only about twelve feet, so I could see the dark area on the hardwood floor where she had bled out.

"Can Carrie call in a cleaner yet?" Some cleaners specialized in sanitizing biohazardous areas—anything from sewage-soaked carpets from overflowing toilets to bloody crime scenes. Unlike in the movies, these cleaners didn't show up on their own. It was the responsibility of family and friends to hire someone to do it. Since Carrie was in the hospital, she probably hadn't even thought about it.

"We finished up here yesterday," Reese acknowledged. "She can have someone come in now."

"I'll let her know." When she got out of the hospital, it would be hard enough dealing with her mother's funeral arrangements. The last thing she needed was to come here to find Dolly an outfit for the funeral home and walk into this horror. "If she can't make the call herself, I'll do it for her."

"They moved Carrie out of intensive care this morning." Reese cringed as she added, "I got a look at her arm when they changed the bandages out last night. I don't know how they managed to save her hand."

Reese was in her late twenties. They didn't interact much at the baby shower, and I'd never heard Reese mention her, so it hadn't dawned on me that she and Carrie might be friends. "How long have you known Carrie?"

"As long as anyone knows anyone in a small town. She was two grades ahead of me, so we didn't hang out, but I was aware of her."

The way she'd described her relationship with Carrie made me feel like Reese was holding something back.

Ezra must have picked up on it as well because he asked her, "Is there something more?"

"Not really." Reese wiggled her mouth as her brow lowered. "There were rumors about Carrie and one of the high school teachers her senior year." Her expression was one of consternation. "The thing is, I never believed it. It doesn't have anything to do with what's going on now, anyway. So that's why I didn't say anything."

Her response seemed to mollify Ezra. "Okay. We're here," he said. "Nora, do your thing."

I raised my brows. "My thing, huh?"

"You know what I mean."

"I certainly do." Ezra and Reese followed me into the living room. I went over to the box on the shelf. "Did you guys go through this?"

Reese nodded. "I checked it out when you first told me about it."

I opened the small chest and took out the ring. "I think the man in my vision, Dodger, gave this ring to Dolly." I showed Ezra the inscription. "He said this to her. That he'd been right here waiting for her?"

"Like the old Richard Marx song," Ezra said.

"Who?" Reese asked.

I rolled my eyes so hard. "Only a multiplatinum artist of awesome ballads like *Should've Known Better*, *Hold On To The Nights*, and of course, *Right Here Waiting*."

She snickered. "I'll take your word for it."

Reese McKay didn't know it yet, but the next time we had a girls' night out, she was going to get a music education. I scoped out the living room and wasn't picking up any strong odors. "I can't believe she doesn't even have any scented candles in this place."

"Some people don't like them," Reese said defensively.

"Would some people, be you?" I asked.

She looked chagrined. "Possibly."

I walked through the kitchen. The scent of alcohol had faded, and I couldn't detect any aromas that triggered my gift.

"Okay, so these are the only two rooms I was in before. You said she had an office?"

"What about the bathroom?" Ezra asked.

I gave him a bland look. "I don't love the things I see when it comes to other people's bathrooms."

His chest vibrated as he suppressed a chortle. "Still, you should probably—"

"Fine, fine," I said. "I will sniff the toilet." I shook my head. "Not literally. I will not be sticking my nose down by the commode. There is only so much, as a good citizen, that I'm willing to do."

"That's fair," he said.

Reese, who was behind me, let out a tittering giggle that ended in a snort.

The bathroom was as neat as the rest of the house, and Dolly's soaps and lotions were hypoallergenic and scent-free. "I think she might have had allergies to more than just snake venom," I said.

Ezra put his hand on the door frame and leaned in. "Did you get a hit on something?"

"The opposite," I said with relief. "There are no scents to be had in here. Let's tackle the office next." I wasn't holding out high hopes, though. So far, the only aromas that held any strong memories for Dolly had been related to alcohol.

Which gave me an idea. "What did you do with that bottle of vodka?"

"It's behind the seat of my truck," Ezra said. "Do you want me to get it?"

"I think it might help."

He didn't even question why as he took off to get the bottle. I loved that about him.

Reese waited until he was out of earshot, then said, "It might help me, too."

"Not for the drinking," I countered.

"But for the stinking," she finished.

I gave her a playful nudge. "We're poets who should never quit our day jobs."

"Never," she concurred.

It didn't take Ezra long to get back. He handed me the bottle. "What happens now?"

"We shall see." Reese led the way to Dolly's office. It was wall-to-wall vintage chic décor. The walls were a bright yellow, with blue and green chunky accent shelves, including several needlepoints of vintage dolls framed behind her desk. The room's clutter was a complete dichotomy to the tidier living spaces at the front of her home.

I unscrewed the cap of the vodka bottle and moved the opening to just below my nose.

A woman with gray hair sits at a desk in a room I immediately recognize as Dolly's office. She is crying as she opens the desk drawer and takes out a bottle of vodka. She stares at it for a moment, then opens it, breaking the seal. I see her head bob up and down, and she is muttering a prayer. She tightens the lid and pushes the bottle aside.

She gets up and stands in front of a needlepoint of two dolls holding hands with the words, "Friends are never far apart when you keep them in your heart." She lifts the frame from the nail in the wall and sets it down on her desk. She grabs a box cutter that I didn't see before and whistles sadly as she pushes the blade into the sheetrock and starts to cut.

When the memory ended, Ezra stood beside me, his hand cupping my elbow. Both he and Reese were staring at me with anticipation.

"Well?" Reese asked. "Any joy?"

I made my way to the friendship needlepoint and lifted it from the wall. On the other side was a ragged square hole in the wall. I smiled at Reese. "We have joy."

I got out of the way as Reese put on gloves and examined the contents of the recess. "There are at least fifteen thousand dollars in here, and there's a gold ring with a green gemstone." She held the ring up to the light. "It says fourteen k, so fourteen karat gold."

"If that's a real emerald, it's a big freaking stone," I said. "It's probably worth at least ten thousand dollars or more."

"Why would she stash cash and a ring in her wall?" Reese mused.

As I stared at the hole in the sheetrock, I had a fair idea of why. "The jewelry and bank thieves, David Summers and that Tracy guy that died, you said there was a third partner that got away? That Summers wouldn't give up."

Ezra's eyes widened as he put the pieces together at the same time as me. "You don't think Dolly…"

"It's the only thing that makes sense," I told him. "I think we found the robber that got away."

CHAPTER 19

*A*fter the secret hidey-hole reveal, Ezra and Reese called our outing officially closed as they brought in a team to search the house from top to bottom. By the time the police were done with the new search, the gorgeous A-Frame house would be a mess. But I'd make sure Carrie had access to all the help she needed to put it back together.

Talk about the sins of a parent coming back to haunt the child. In the past four months, she'd found out her father was a convicted murderer. She gets bit by a snake, her mother dies, and now her mom might have been as guilty of felony murder as her biological dad? It would be enough to make the Dalai Lama lose his Zen.

Officer Jeanna Thompson, who I knew from my previous work with the police department, was tasked with driving me back to town.

"Thanks, Jeanna," I said when she dropped me off.

"Come into the shop sometime, and I'll gift you some goodies."

"I don't think we're allowed to take gifts, Ms. Black," she replied politely.

"I won't tell if you don't."

"And that's how good cops go bad." Her deadpan response took me aback. Until she cracked a smile and gave me a quick wave goodbye. "It was nice to see you again, ma'am. Have a nice day."

"You too, Officer Thompson."

I let my car warm up for a minute before my short drive from Dolly's shop to mine. Gilly and Pippa were hanging out in the small waiting area of the massage room.

"Slow morning?" I asked.

"My eight and nine o'clock canceled," Gilly said. "It gets a little cold outside, and people don't want to leave their homes. Not even for a nice warm massage."

"If you want a client, I'll take the slot," I offered. This morning's visions had taken it out of me.

"I always have an opening for you," Gilly said. She got up from her seat and gave me the most formidable, bestest hug, and I felt my body sag with relief.

When she let me go, I gave her a grateful smile. "I needed that."

"I know. Let me go turn on the bed warmer, and we'll get started."

I noticed we were missing a person. "Hey, Tippi didn't come in with you today?"

"No, she's helping Jordy out at the coffee shop. Turns out for a spoiled princess, she makes a decent barista."

"You needed the break," I said.

"I sure did." Pippa winced and put her hand under her stomach.

"Are you okay?"

"The doctor says it's Braxton-Hicks contractions. I've been getting them off and on all week. If this is a fake contraction, I'm scared of what the real ones are like."

I got her a lavender scented neck pillow, and she put it behind her head.

"It's not been too bad, though, right? Your sister seems like she sincerely wants to connect with you."

"I want to believe her motives are pure, Nora, but I've been bamboozled by her before. Every time I find myself relaxing my guard, she says or does something that brings back our old issues. I want to believe she's changed, but it's hard to turn off that part of my brain that still sees her as the party girl who doesn't care who she hurts as long as she's having fun."

I thought about the memory I'd had of her and a guy named Jackie. He'd loved her, but he'd still left her for his own survival and healing. "Whatever happens, just know that you are awesome, and it's okay to feel what you're feeling."

Gilly opened the door. "Ready, Freddie."

"Hey, do either of you want to go to an alcoholics anonymous meeting with me tonight at the White Rose Church?"

"I drink way more than you do, Nora. You don't have a problem," Gilly said.

"I appreciate the vote of confidence, but I'm not going for me. Dolly was in AA, and I want to see if she attended the church meetings. And if she did, I need to find out who her sponsor was."

Pippa leaned forward in her seat. "I want to go. Jordy's meetings are all closed, but I would like to see what these meetings are all about."

I nodded. "The more, the merrier. What about Tippi?"

Pippa frowned. "She says she's made a friend and is going out tonight."

"She's only been in town a few days," Gilly said.

Pippa waved her hand as if shooing a fly. "I told you the girl works fast. Her going out with a stranger tonight is the exact reason I'm finding it difficult to trust her."

"Well, we'll make it a girls' night then. The meeting starts at seven, and we can get something to eat before." My enthusiasm was high. "We haven't done something with just the three of us in so long."

"If taking us to an AA meeting gets you this excited, we really do need a girls' night. A proper one," Gilly said.

* * *

WE CLOSED the shop early again, and I drove straight home and got in the shower. Between the massage and several sweaty hot flashes, I was officially on the hot mess express. After I got dressed in a light T-shirt and jeans, I called my doctor and got an appointment for next week. I'd had my hysterectomy last January. It was February now, so I was late for my one-year checkup anyhow.

Ezra had called to tell me they didn't find any more money or jewels at Dolly's house, and they were going to do a thorough search of her business in the afternoon. There was no way to confirm whether or not she was part of David Summers' crew, especially with the other participants dead. Still, I had a feeling the blackmail was related to those long-ago robberies. Dolly wouldn't have wanted her daughter to know about her shady past. I wonder if she felt as if she'd disappointed her daughter enough for one lifetime.

Even with all the clues, I couldn't figure out who would have blackmailed Dolly. It could be anyone, and I wouldn't know because my ding dang sniffer-vision was always out of focus. The man's voice didn't sound familiar, but why would it? Unless it was Ezra or another man I knew well, like Jordy, I'm not sure I could distinguish one voice from another. There hadn't been any distinct accent either, just a general Midwest, no-frills tone. The only thing I felt good about was that I'd managed to uncover a significant get for Ezra and Reese. I'd proven their faith in me.

A few hours later, I was with my two best buds, Gilly driving, and stomachs full on Taco Shake Shack tacos and shakes. It sent a thrill through me the way it had when we were teens. I had to fight the urge not to stick my head out the window and scream to the world that I was here, and I wasn't going anywhere.

"You have got the biggest smile on your face," Gilly said. "You're beaming."

"She's probably thinking about Detective Hot Stuff," Pippa teased from the backseat.

"Actually, I'm happy to be here in this vehicle with my two best friends while we cruise the strip."

Gilly giggled. "I'm not sure driving to White Rose Church is considered cruising the strip." She bopped me with her elbow. "But I get your drift."

"There it is," Pippa said. She pointed up ahead toward a yellow neon cross with a white neon rose at the center. "Their signage is a little on the nose."

"Makes it easy to find," I said. It was dark out, but the church's small parking lot was well lit. About a dozen cars and trucks took up the closest spots to the building. Gilly circled the lot three times. "Just park," I said.

"I want to be close to the church, but under a light," she said.

I rolled my eyes. "It's not going to happen."

"I'll protect you, Gils," Pippa said. "Baby Davenport-Hines has a mean karate kick. No bad guys stand a chance."

"I'm not worried about us. This car is only a year old. I don't want anyone accidentally damaging her."

"Then you should have let Nora drive," Pippa said.

"I prefer to be in control," Gilly responded.

"Then be in control and park," I said. "At this rate, the meeting will be over before we get out of the car."

"Fine." Gilly huffed. "Parking."

She picked a spot near the highway entrance that was

still close to the church. "There."

As we were walking inside, still laughing about Gilly's need to be in charge, I saw paramedic Grant go inside the front doors.

"It looks like we're going to know at least one person in there tonight," I said.

When we got inside, the church walls were stark white with black and brown trim. There were paper arrows taped at various locations down two corridors, pointing the way to the meeting, along with several signs saying things like *All our welcome in my house, sayeth the Lord.*

As we rounded a corner into a large room with tile floors, I smelled the acidic aroma of cheap coffee. The refreshment table consisted of a coffee maker, a water cooler, paper coffee cups, and two plates of cookies. From the aroma, the coffee had been brewed using stale coffee grinds, but the cookies, which were Neapolitans with perfect white, pink, and brown stripes, looked delicious. Along the wall were folded up tables, a basket of balls and rackets, reams of paper, and other assorted bits and bobbles for crafting and exercise. In the center of the room were eight rows of metal folding chairs. Most everyone was seated. I watched Grant take his seat in the second row between a blonde woman and a man in a suit. There were probably eighteen people in attendance, not including my BFF brigade.

"Let's sit in the back," Pippa said in a hushed tone.

"Sounds good." I let Pippa sit on the outside chair just in case Junior kicked her bladder, and she needed to make a break for the bathroom. Gilly took the seat on the other side of me.

Pippa rubbed her hands together. "I'm a little nervous." She had a smile on her face, so I knew it was more excitement than apprehension.

A man said, "No, need to be nervous. Is this your first time?"

We all turned and looked behind us at the same time and saw it was Bob, the paramedic.

"Bob," I said.

He put his finger to his lips. "It's supposed to be anonymous." He cracked a smile. "I'm kidding. Whatever reason you ladies are here, it's nice to see you outside an emergency."

"Agreed," I said.

Hmm. So, Bob was an alcoholic. I wondered how long he'd been sober. Not that it mattered. We were in a room of people trying to keep their lives in order, and in the grand scheme of things, isn't that something we all wanted?

"Maybe we should go," Gilly said. "It's weird knowing people here and not, you know, being alcoholics."

"I looked it up. The public is welcome to open meetings." I patted her knee. "All the people who came tonight are aware of that, so stop worrying."

"Okay," she said. "I'll try to remain calm."

I watched Bob walk to the front of the chairs and turn to face the group. He smiled warmly. "Hi, I'm Bob. I'm an alcoholic."

"Hi, Bob," several people replied.

"It's my birthday. Thank you to my beautiful wife Nana for my cookies." He held up a chip. "As of today, I've been eighteen years sober."

There was a light round of applause.

"I'm happy to have my family here tonight, my wife, my son, and his wife to support me. And it's so nice to see other new faces in here tonight. While this is a meeting place, a safe space for people who wish to stop drinking, tonight's meeting is open to anyone who wants to know more about Alcoholics Anonymous and our mission. I'll start the meeting with a reading of our preamble."

"See," I told Gilly. "Anyone can come tonight."

She let out a slow breath. "Okay."

Bob finished the preamble, then said, "As a group, we recite the serenity prayer. If you aren't religious, you don't have to, but it's a good message, even if you're not a believer. It's about giving up the idea of controlling things that are beyond your control."

Pippa leaned across my lap and whispered to Gilly, "You need this prayer."

I swallowed my laugh, but Pippa wasn't wrong. Although, maybe giving up a little control was something all three of us could stand.

"Now," Bob said after the prayer was finished. "We'll be doing some readings from *Twelve Steps and Twelve Traditions*, which gives us all a greater understanding of the program and how it works.

Fifteen minutes and several readings later, Bob asked, "Does anyone want to share your experience with the group tonight? Something that has given you hope or strength?"

I watched the blonde get up and slide past Grant and the tall man as she made her way to the front of the room. Bob gave her a hug, said something quietly in her ear, then nodded as she turned around.

It was all I could do to stop my jaw from landing in my lap as Pippa's younger sister stood before the group and said, "Hi, my name is Tippi, and I'm an alcoholic."

The room said, "Hi, Tippi."

Pippa grabbed my hand in a tight grip. As painful as it was, I didn't stop her.

Tippi looked down at her hands as she fidgeted with a coin. "I haven't had a drink in two months."

The group clapped for her.

"I...coming to Garden Cove, I didn't know what to expect. I've been running away from my life for so long. My drinking drove away my friends. Drove away the one man who loved me for me. And I worry that it's ruined my chance to reconcile with my sister. Someone I've always looked up to, and I've been nothing but a disappointment. Not drinking is hard."

There were a few titters of laughter through the room.

Tippi forced a smile. "But being alone is harder." She looked up and saw us. Her face paled as she dropped her arms to her sides. But she cleared her throat and kept going.

"I have hope that I can make a new life for myself. One that doesn't involve dependency. I've seen how good life can be when you say no to drinking and yes to every-thing else." She finished, cast her eyes down, and returned to her seat.

Pippa had tears in her eyes. She released my hand so she could dig in her purse for a tissue. My fingers were numb from her grip, and I stretched them out to restart the circulation.

Bob resumed his role as leader. "Anyone else want to share?"

When no one came forward, Bob asked that everyone stand up, come to the open area, and hold hands for the Lord's prayer.

Pippa got up and walked to Tippi. She held out her hand to her sister. Tippi smiled through tears as she locked fingers with Pippa.

Grant was on the other side, and I wanted to get close to him to see if I could get any memories. There was something about the kid that bothered me. I was so focused on him that I bumped into another guy who was heading toward the doors.

"Excuse me," he said.

My focus was on Grant, so I barely looked at him. "Sorry," I said automatically.

"Nora?" the man said. "Did you just start coming here?"

"Davis." The man who had bumped me was Marjorie Meadow's son. "I...this is my first time."

"Well, welcome to AA," he said. "It works if you keep working it." On that sage note, he headed out of the meeting.

CHAPTER 20

I hung out in the back near the coffee and cookies table. I was still in the back as the meeting finished up. They ended with *Keep coming back. It works if you work it.*

I remembered Jordy saying that Dolly probably had a female sponsor. But other than Tippi, my BFFs, and Bob's wife, I didn't see any other women in the group. Pippa and Gilly talked to Bob at the treat table. Tippi helped Grant and a few others put away the folding chairs, stacking them against the wall.

Their conversation seemed more casual friendly than flirty, so I grabbed a chair and joined them. "Hey, Tippi."

Grant walked away before I could greet him as well. I thought for sure he'd seen me, but maybe he was uncomfortable about talking to me.

"Hey." Tippi's expression was a combination of happiness and uncertainty. "I can't believe you, Pippa, and Gilly are here tonight."

"I'm sorry if we messed up your night. We didn't know you'd be here."

"Jordy told me about the meetings. I've needed one all week," she said. "Back home, I was going to five meetings a week, so this week has been the first in two months that I hadn't had almost daily support."

I glanced at Pippa. "I think you'll have a lot more support now."

Tippi raised a brow and smiled conspiratorially. "Is it bad that I'm glad she's here? I was going to tell her about me working the program, but I worried she wouldn't believe me, and it's easy to spin out."

"Pippa is one of the best people I know. If you're sincere, she'll come around."

"That's good news for me, then." She smiled, and I could see the resemblance to Pippa so clearly. "I'm going to ask her if I can stick around a while longer. Do you think she'll let me?"

Pippa would most likely say yes, but I wasn't about to commit my girl to a houseguest. However, with the baby coming soon, maybe Tippi sticking around wouldn't be such a terrible idea. On the other hand, she was a newly recovering alcoholic. She waited patiently for my response, and I finally settled on, "All you can do is ask."

I could tell it wasn't exactly the encouragement she'd been hoping for, but she nodded. "I will keep my expectations low, but my hopes high."

I chuckled. "Good plan. Do you need a ride home?"

"Do you mind? Jordy hooked me up with Grant for a ride over, but I'll let him know that I have a ride home."

Since I wasn't sure I trusted Grant as much as Jordy, I said, "Another good plan." Grant took the last chair and was walking it toward the wall. I still held the one I'd grabbed. "I'll come get you when we get ready to go." I wiggled the chair. "I better put this up."

Unlike with Davis, I accidentally, on purpose, bumped into the young man.

"Oh, hey," he said. "Sorry." His shoulders were rounded forward and slightly slumped. "Let me take that." He put his hands on the chair. The unmistakable aroma of fresh tobacco smoke clung to his clothing.

A man sits in a chair circle, holding an unlit cigarette as he bounces his knee. He's wearing pale blue pants and a white short-sleeved shirt. "Man, I just don't want to be here anymore," he says.

Seven other men, also wearing pale blue pants and white shirts, sit in the circle. The floor is concrete, and the walls are blue. Is this a prison?

"Who does?" one of the other men asks with evident annoyance. "This ain't a country club. You ain't supposed to like it."

The man who complained scoots forward in his seat and dips his head. I see a spade tattoo behind his ear. It's Grant. "When I get out," he says. "I'm never coming back."

"Sure, pal," another one of the men says. "None of us are coming back." The statement is met with laughter.

"You okay, Ms. Black?" Grant asked. "You look like you spaced there for a minute."

"I'm...yep, okay. It's nice to see you again."

He took the chair I was carrying. "I'll put this up for you."

I nodded and let him go. If Grant had done a stint in jail, I wanted to find out why before I poked at him. I didn't think a person could have a dangerous criminal record, though, and be an EMT. They probably did all kinds of background checks, so it was probably a non-violent conviction. Of course, this was all supposition on my part. Heck, what I saw could have been Grant being scared straight. He was a young man, and that vision could have been several years old.

I joined Pippa and Gilly at the cookies.

"These are delicious," Gilly said as she bit into one of the Neapolitans. "Nom nom."

"My wife made them special for me. They're my favorite," Bob told her. "Anyhow, usually cake is served for big birthdays, but these are better as far as I'm concerned.

"Happy birthday," I said. Then frowned. "Is that appropriate?"

Bob chuckled. "Yep. Totally appropriate." He glanced across the room over my head. "Oops. My wife is waving at me. Better go."

I looked at my two BFFs, both with cookie crumbs at the corners of their lips. "It appears that tonight has been a bust as far as Dolly is concerned, but it seems like you two are making the most of it."

Pippa finished chewing. "Dolly did come to meetings here for a little while years ago, but she'd started attending meetings in another town. Bob says that's normal for recovering alcoholics who want to really keep anonymous. Apparently, about ninety percent of the members of this group are from Rasfield."

Okay, that made a lot of sense. "So, Dolly probably attended meetings over there."

"Exactly." Pippa nodded, her expression just a wee bit smug. "Yep. Who's the bust now?"

Gilly looked at Pippa's ever-growing boobs. "It used to be me, but lately, it's been a lot you."

I reached out and brushed the crumbs from Gilly's cheek. "You're both the bust," I said.

We stayed for about ten minutes more, talking to a few of the attendees. The coffee and sweets made the table a high traffic area. I'd had several scent-memory bombs, but since none of them had anything to do with Dolly, I did as Jordy had asked, and I put them in the never-tell vault.

After a while, the emotional layers started to wear heavily on me. "I'm ready to call it a night," I said. "Why don't we grab Tippi and get out of here?"

* * *

THE NEXT DAY, I called it at eleven o'clock. "This week has been ridiculously slow," I said. The sidewalks had been salted, but there were still mounds of snow from a freak blizzard the previous night.

"Well, if mother nature would quit crapping glitter on our parade, more customers would be willing to come out," Gilly said.

"I don't want to go home," Pippa lamented. "Jordy and

Tippi are working, and I love our puppers, but Bo wants to go in and out constantly, especially now that there's snow on the ground. Do you know how hard it is to get up and down constantly in my condition?"

I smirked. "I do not."

She gave me a contrite look. "I'm sorry, Nora, I didn't mean—"

"Please don't apologize. I don't want to have my own children. You know this about me. Until my hysterectomy, I actively took measures to prevent pregnancies." I laughed. "I will love your baby to kingdom come, but I promise you, I will not regret my own choice not to have one. Besides, I love being an aunt. I get to spoil and love without all the diapers and crying."

"And you're a wonderful aunt," Gilly said. "Ari and Marco love you so much."

I put my hand on her shoulder. "And bonus, they will always think I'm way cooler than you."

"They are the only ones who think that," Gilly said.

I winked at Pippa. "Mark my word, when the time comes, Baby Davenport-Hines will think I'm cooler than you, too."

"I'm sorry," she said again. "I know all this about you, but hormones can turn your brain to cake. If we were busier, I'd have less time to manufacture drama."

"We're so lucky we have the Nurse Mary contracts," Gilly added. "So many businesses are struggling."

A proverbial lightbulb lit up in my head. "Let's go shopping. We'll close up and head down the strip. I get a chance to wear my super cute coat—"

"It is adorable," Pippa interjected.

"And we'll buy things from every shop that's open on the street today," I finished. "It won't keep anyone afloat financially, but it'll be an act of kindness on top of being fun."

"Are you sure you want to do all that walking?" Gilly asked Pippa.

"It's a couple of blocks up and down the street," she said. "I'll be fine. Oh, can we go to Bodacious Boutique? I need some new stretchy pants."

I didn't judge her. I wasn't pregnant and liked a good stretchy pant to lounge in. "We have our first stop."

Fifteen minutes later, we closed the shop and started on our shopping spree. The Bodacious Boutique was across the street and one block over on the left side. The gentle tinkle of the doorbell alerted the owner Monica Powers to our presence.

"Come in, ladies," she said. "Let me know if I can help you find something."

"Thanks, Monica," Pippa said. "I know exactly what I want."

She made a beeline to a rack of leggings. She grabbed a light blue pair, a yellow patterned pair, and a pair in black. I grabbed a black pair as well, and Gilly took one that was chocolate brown with beige pinstripes. After we browsed a few minutes more, I added a cornflower blue sweater to my purchase.

"You all come again," Monica said after checking us out. "And thanks for dropping by. You're the first customers I've had in two days."

We said our goodbyes and then headed to our next destination.

"I want some walnut fudge." Gilly pointed at Beets' Treats across the road. "It's the weather for it, don't you think?"

The neon open sign was lit, which surprised me since Jane had been robbed a couple days earlier. I would have been scared to be in the shop alone if that had happened to me. Still, I was happy to get anything chocolate.

I gave Gilly a quick grin. "Beets' Treats it is."

There wasn't any traffic, so we jaywalked across the street instead of going to the end of the block to the crossing.

Pippa wiggled her hips as she did her best bad impression of Matthew McConaughey in the first *Magic Mike*. "We're lawbreakers."

Gilly chortled. "Someone call the cops. We're going to jail."

Jail made me think of Grant. I wanted so badly to ask Ezra to search the young man for his record, but my promise to Jordy kept me silent. What I'd seen had nothing to do with Dolly, and so I shoved it back in the vault again. "We would run the cell block."

"You mean we'd be doing a lot of running away. Brrrrr." Pippa shivered. "I didn't realize how biting the wind was."

Beets' Treats was wonderfully warm and smelled yummy.

Jane's display case had three shelves with five different types of confections and baked sweets on each one of them—cookies, fudges, chocolate toffee, brownies, and brittle, and I was here for each and every one of them.

"Welcome," Jane greeted. "What can I get for you?"

"Uhm, one of everything," I said. "It all looks so delicious."

Pippa oofed and bent forward. "I think Baby Davenport-Hines wants everything as well, and he's willing to kick his way out to get it."

"Do you need to sit down?" Jane asked, her face a myriad of concern.

"Actually," Pippa said. "I could use the bathroom."

"Of course." Jane waved at her. "Come on around the display here, and I'll take you back."

I put my arm around Pippa to help steady her in case Junior went in for the kill. "Maybe this was a bad idea."

"This was an awesome idea," Pip said. "But I am giving birth to a party pooper."

"There will certainly be a lot of poop," Gilly agreed.

We followed Jane into the magical land of her kitchen filled with the heavenly ambrosia of vanilla, chocolate, hazelnuts, peppermint, and more.

A woman kneels on the floor and punches eight numbers into a circular panel. The top opens. It's a floor safe. I've seen them before. She empties the small amount of cash from it and shoves it in her purse. Next, she runs to the back of the kitchen and unlocks the door. She knocks a few pans on the floor before she starts hyperventilating herself with sharp, quick breaths.

When she's good and worked up, she says, "Help, I've been

robbed. I've been robbed." She puts on her coat, grabs her purse, then runs.

Oh, no. No, no. This was one vision I wished I could send back.

Jane Beets had faked the break-in at her store.

CHAPTER 21

"**Y**ou have to tell, Ezra, right?" Gilly said. "We're all living scared because of these robberies, and to find out that Jane faked hers?" She made a growly sound. "That just chaps my butt."

"But does she?" Pippa asked. "I mean, we know how much Jane's been struggling. Do we really want to ruin her life over one tiny lie?"

Gilly balled her fists on her hips. "Jane lied to *us*. We're practically accomplices."

"I wouldn't go that far," I said. "Other than my stinky vision, I don't have any proof Jane set up her own robbery."

"But you're still going to tell Ezra," Gilly said.

I nodded and gave Pippa a look that I hope conveyed that I was sorry that I couldn't take her side on this. "It's not like he'll arrest Jane on the spot. He'll investigate. And he'll only charge her if he finds evidence that she set up a fake theft for an insurance payout."

"Nora, c'mon," said Pippa. "It's not like she is claiming that much money was stolen."

"Desperation makes people do stupid things," I said. "But sometimes, it reveals character. I like Jane, but I don't know her extremely well. It might not be the first time she's told a so-called harmless lie." I thought about Dolly Paris. Sweet, middle-aged doll collector who wouldn't hurt a fly. Except she had been a fugitive. And a man had died during one of several robberies her crew committed.

Gilly crossed her arms over her chest as we walked back to Scents & Scentsability. "It's not harmless, and it's not about her trying to con money out of her insurance company. I've been scared this week. Between the snake, finding Dolly dead, and *actual* armed bandits, I've had to talk myself out of confining my kids to the house."

Pippa, who was a little ahead of us with her long stride, stopped abruptly and turned. She and Gilly locked gazes. For a second, I thought the two of them were going to fight. Instead, Pippa put her arms around Gilly and gave her a good long hug. "I'm sorry," she said. "You deserve to feel safe. We all do."

Marjorie Meadows, her son Davis, and a guy I didn't recognize walked up the sidewalk toward us. Marjorie had on a full-length parka with a fur hood, seriously decked out for our winter weather.

"Nora. Just the woman I wanted to see." She slipped on a slick ice spot, and Davis grasped her arm and held her up.

"Be careful, Ma," Davis said. "I told you we should

have driven." He met my gaze but didn't mention seeing me last night, so I didn't either.

"Nonsense," she told him. The other man softly chuckled. He had on a thick coat, a beanie, and sunglasses. "Nora, this is Christopher Staten, the up-and-coming artist whose show I'm sponsoring tomorrow night."

I nodded to him. "Congratulations."

"Thank you," he said with an accent I couldn't quite place. If I had to guess, I'd call it faux-French with a touch of Monty Python. "Marjorie's patronage has meant the world to me."

If Marjorie had been a male peacock, feathers would have been sticking straight up. "You are all coming, I hope."

"We're planning on it," I said.

Gilly muttered, "As long as you're not inviting any criminals."

"What did you say, dear?" Marjorie asked.

"Nothing," Gilly said. "It's a hypothetical debate as to whether you should turn someone in for a crime they've committed, even if you have no proof."

That wasn't exactly the debate.

I raised my brow at Gilly, and she sighed. "I apologize." She made it a blanket statement. "It's been a rough week."

"I do understand," Marjorie said. "Between Dolly and all the robberies in town, I've been anxious as well. Especially now that Davis has sold one of Christopher's pieces already." She gesticulated her excitement. "I didn't have any faith in those online auctions, but I think my son might have saved the gallery with his innovative thinking."

Online auctions had been around for a couple of decades, so it wasn't all that innovative. However, I did agree that it was smart. "I've been looking up some of those auctions. I have to say, art lovers are willing to spend money."

"Good art will always attract good patrons," Marjorie agreed. "Well, we have a few more stops this afternoon. I'm counting on all of you tomorrow night. Jane is going to be fashioning desserts that look like art as well. That'll be so much fun."

At Jane's name, Gilly rolled her eyes. I grasped her by the arm before she could start talking about criminals again. "We should get going as well. Tomorrow night, then. Nice to meet you, Christopher. And good luck on the auctions." I tipped my head to Davis. "I wish you many sales."

The below-freezing temperatures were starting to seep into my bones. I picked up the pace until we were back inside the shop. "I don't think I'll ever be warm again." I kept my coat and mittens on as I sat in the waiting area.

Pippa plopped down next to me. She scooted a magazine rack over and put her feet on it. "My internal heater is raging," she said. "But my fingers feel like they might fall off. Who thought it was a good idea to do all that walking?"

Gilly retrieved hot pads from her warmer and gave

me and Pippa one, then she grabbed one for herself before sitting down in the last chair available. "I'm sorry for being bitchy."

"Me too," Pippa said.

They both looked at me as if waiting for me to say I was sorry as well. I gave them both a bland look. "I accept your apologies."

"I still think Nora should report this to Ezra," Gilly said.

"Which she will do," I said, referring to myself in the third person. "I mean, I will."

"I know it's the right thing to do," Pippa admitted. "It's just that I like Jane."

"I like her too." Gilly reached across my lap and put her hand on Pippa's. "We're good, right?"

Pippa stacked her free hand on top of Gilly's. "We're the bust."

I slipped my hand out from the blessed warmth of the heating pad to top off their stack. "The bustiest ever," I told them.

ON THE WAY home that afternoon, I stopped at the hospital to see Carrie. Reese had said she'd been moved out of intensive care, and the help desk told me she was in Room 102B in the post-critical care ward. It was on the first floor of the hospital in the east wing.

I knocked at the open door.

"Come in." Carrie was sitting up in a bedside recliner.

A pitcher of water, a cup with ice and a straw, and a box of tissue on the overbed table, which was currently over the chair. It was amazing how much better she looked. Her fingers were still purple, and her forearm was wrapped from wrist to elbow, but she was out of the sling.

"How are you feeling?"

"Physically, much better." She wiggled her fingers on the snake-bit side. "I'm even getting some feeling back. The doctor thinks I'll make a full recovery."

"Wonderful!" I said enthusiastically. Carrie had needed some good news this week. "When do you get to go home?"

"They tell me I might get to go home in the morning."

"More good news." I sat on the side of her bed nearest the chair. "Do you have a ride home? I'm happy to pick you up."

She tilted her head at me and smiled. "I have a friend picking me up."

I wondered if it was the young paramedic Grant. I couldn't quite nail down if he was a good guy or not. Maybe if he didn't act like he was avoiding me every time I ran into him, I would feel differently. But it's hard to trust someone who rarely made eye contact. So I used the opportunity to ask, "Is your friend that handsome EMT?"

Carrie tucked her hair behind her ear and smiled. "How did you know?"

"I saw him visit you the other day. It seemed above and beyond the call of duty. Have you known him long?"

Carrie nodded. "Grant and I started seeing each other about six months ago, but I knew him from..." She pressed her lips together into a thin line then released them with a soft *pah* sound. "When I was a teenager, I had a teacher who helped kids like me. He ran an Alateen group, you know, for teenagers with parents who drink. Mom had gotten sober by then, but I'd been conditioned to certain behaviors that were not in my own best interest." She smiled sardonically. "My mom had raised an enabler. Mr. Parsons, who had been in Al-Anon, reached out to me." Carrie blinked at me. "He saved my life."

"And Grant?"

"He was a member of Mr. Parsons' group. Only, it was his father who drank. We became friends of a sort. Birds of a feather, and all that. He stopped going to meetings about the middle of my senior year. I never knew what happened to him until we ran into each other last year."

I wondered if she knew he had been in jail. I couldn't ask because of my promise to Jordy, but it didn't stop me from hoping she would volunteer the information.

"He got into some trouble when he was eighteen," Carrie explained.

Hope lived. "What kind of trouble?"

"I don't want you to judge him. Grant had a difficult life. His father was abusive, and both he and his mother suffered."

"We all have pasts, Carrie. All that matters is what you do in the present." And I really wanted to know what the heck Grant was up to right now.

"He got drunk and stole his dad's car."

Okay. Not quite the bad boy tale I'd expected. "That's a teenager acting out."

She squinted and wrinkled her nose. "It gets worse. He ran the car into the side of a pawn shop and stole some stuff."

"Jewelry?" I blurted.

Carrie gave me an arch look, and I forced myself to appear calm.

"I mean, what did he take?"

"Some watches," she admitted. "But, also, a gun. He went to jail for a few years. After he got out, he moved to Arkansas and started over.

"Why did he move back home?"

"His mom finally divorced his dad. He moved back to help her."

"Your mom didn't approve of you seeing him?"

Carrie shook her head sadly. "She saw him at one of her AA meetings and heard his story. She didn't want me to fall in love with someone she called a liar and a thief."

"I'm sorry, Carrie. That must have been hard to hear."

"I stopped seeing Grant for a little while, other than as friends. Until I found out about my biological dad. I realized Mom had been scared I was falling for a guy like him, but Grant is nothing like that."

"How did Grant feel about your mom trying to come between you two?"

"He didn't like it." She narrowed a suspicious gaze on me. "He didn't kill her if that's what you're implying. He's the kindest person I know, and he doesn't have a violent bone in his body. He withdraws from conflict. The one-time he acted out, he paid dearly for it. I promise you, Nora, Grant didn't do it."

"I'm not accusing Grant." I kept my tone comfortable and calm. Because there wasn't enough evidence at this point to accuse anyone. Still, it seemed awfully coincidental that Grant was a thief. Maybe he was innocent. I hoped so, for Carrie's sake.

"Good, because Grant loves me. He wouldn't do anything to hurt me, and losing Mom is the worst pain I've ever felt." She looked down at her bandaged arm. "The worst pain."

"I didn't mean to upset you," I said with sympathy. "That wasn't my intention."

She was silent for a moment as she gathered her thoughts. "I believe you, Nora. Thank you for your kindness this past week. It means a lot."

"Whatever you need," I told her. "It's getting late, and I have dinner plans." With *Bridget Jones: The Edge of Reason* and a pot pie Gilly had made me.

She reached out and stopped just short of touching my arm. "Will you tell Detective Holden? If he says anything about Grant. Tell him he couldn't have done this."

"Do you know if anyone was threatening your mom? Maybe blackmailing her?"

Carrie dropped her hand. "I wish I did. Mom stopped telling me stuff a few months back. I suspected she'd started drinking again, and I avoided her. I couldn't go down that road with her again." She started to weep. "I'm a terrible daughter."

I thought about what Jordy had said about his parents when they cut him out of their lives. "You're a survivor, Carrie, in every way. That makes you admirable, not terrible."

"Thank you, Nora." She dabbed at her eyes and chuckled. "Christ, I always seem to cry when I talk to you."

"Better out than in, my mother always said."

She smiled at me. "Isn't that for burps and farts?"

"Yep." I gave her a sly smile. "But it works for emotions like grief and anger as well."

CHAPTER 22

*J*ordy and Pippa's country home was a rectangle box with red siding. The front of the home was an open floor plan with a large living room, dining room, and kitchen. The sliding glass doors in the kitchen led to a deck overlooking a wooded hill. There were two bedrooms, a master on the left with a private bath and a guest bedroom on the right with a guest bathroom that included a shower.

I'd been over several times since Pippa moved in with Jordy, so I was delighted when Bo, a brindle-colored American Staffordshire, wiggled himself right over to me and turned into my legs so I could give him a thorough butt scratching before he went off to greet everyone else. Jordy had adopted Bo from a shelter in Moonrise, Missouri, a small community near the Bootheel. Helma, the brown, black, and tan basset hound, another rescue from Iowa, was standing out by the cooker with her daddy, hoping he would drop a treat or two. She was slightly overweight and very food motivated, according to Pippa.

Gilly had brought Marco and Ari with her instead of a date. I think she was more hung up on sexy security guard Luke Robson and wasn't as ready to play the field as she wanted us to believe. Ezra had made a beeline to the backyard to huddle around Jordy's new egg-shaped smoker. He and Marco were properly impressed as Jordy explained the fifty gazillion ways he could cook a brisket.

"Just wait, this brisket is going to be tender. It will melt in your mouth!" Jordy called out to us.

"Such dudes," Pippa said. "But I'm thankful Jordy has someone else to explain all the features to."

Gilly giggled.

Tippi rubbed her arms as if to ward off a chill. "It's so cold outside. I can't believe Jordy wants to grill in this cold weather."

"Hah! You underestimate the power that smoked meats have over a man." Pippa's laugh turned into a gasp. She dipped down, holding onto the counter. "Wowza, that was a hard one. I'm fairly sure I peed my pants a little." Her tone was light, but the pain on her face was not.

"Maybe you should skip the gallery opening and take it easy at home," I suggested.

"It's already letting up," she said. "These damn Braxton-Hicks have been hitting me about two to three times a day for the past couple of weeks. The doctor said I shouldn't worry unless they start happening more frequently and with greater intensity."

Tippi opened the lid on the box of glazed twists setting on the breakfast bar that I'd picked up on the way over. It was mine, and Ezra's contribution to the barbeque and the donuts were Pippa's favorites.

"Don't touch my box of donuts." Pippa lightly smacked Tippi's fingers away.

Tippi's lower lip jutted in a pout.

"All right," Pippa said. "You can have a donut. But remember I'm eating for two."

I laughed. "The second person is only the size of a bowling ball."

Pippa wore the pair of black leggings she'd bought the day before with a teal sweater tunic and a pair of low-heeled boots. The tunic was clingy enough to accentuate her large baby bump. She glanced down and said, "I'm almost certain Baby Davenport-Hines is way bigger than a bowling ball."

"Try having twins," Gilly said. "I thought I was going to live through a reenactment of *Alien* where the creature bursts out of the guy's chest."

"I loved that movie," Ari said absently while scrolling her phone. "It's a classic."

Tippi wandered over behind Ari. "What is that?" she asked.

Gilly's face tightened as she waited for Ari to answer.

When her daughter said, "It's an online auction website for art," Gilly let out a little sigh of relief.

"Did you think she was looking at porn, Mom?" I asked.

Gilly's eyes darted between Ari and me. "You never

know what you're going to find when it comes to teenagers, do you? Besides, you know damn well if we'd have had access to naked stuff in the eighties, we would have totally looked."

"We did have access," I said. "*Porky's, Spring Break, Fast Times at Ridgemont High, Bachelor Party.*" The eighties had a slew of movies that were mostly a bunch of T and A. "We saw breasts and booties all the time."

"But no naked men," she pointed out wistfully. "I would have liked to have seen a few more naked men."

I choked on a laugh. "If I recall, you saw a handful of naked men in your misspent youth."

"Ew, Aunt Nora. Gross." Ari said. "Not cool at all."

"Yeah, Nora," Gilly said. "Not cool." She loved Ari's reaction.

"I'm kidding," I amended for the kid's sake. Only I wasn't kidding. Gilly had been a free spirit, and I'd loved that about her from the very start.

"Come look at these, Aunt Nora. There is a painting of three cats with gold leashes on a sidewalk. The description says 786 Cats on fourteen French paving stones bound in gold. Three-point-two weight. The bid is at five thousand and sixty-one dollars."

The amount interested Tippi. "Let me see," she said. "The artist is O.R. Diamante. That's weird."

Pippa came around the breakfast bar to look for herself. "Gold Diamond."

Tippi clapped with enthusiasm. "That's what popped into my head, too. *Or* is French for gold. *Diamant* is French for diamond. I wonder if the artist is French?"

"With that ugly artwork," Pippa said. "I doubt it."

"The titles lack any imagination, but it seems as if people really love them." Gilly had moved around the back of Ari as well until we were all huddled behind the seventeen-year-old.

"Meat is done," Jordy said, as he carried the brisket on a giant serving platter, with Ezra and Marco on either side of him in a makeshift processional for the smoky dish.

Ezra's smile beamed across the kitchen at me. "Look," he said, pointing at the brisket.

"Good," Marco added.

I chuckled at the glee on their faces. "I see. It is good," I agreed. Grilling had turned all three of them into three happy, monosyllabic cavemen, and I was here for it.

"I've got bibs," Pippa said. "About three dozen of them from the baby shower if anyone wants one." She was already tying a mint green terry cloth number around her neck.

I had on a light purple chiffon top. "Yes, please." Gilly, Tippi, and Ari requested their own as well. The boys declined. They were going to be sorry if they ended up with meat stains on their shirts. Ezra brought me over a plate with three thin slices, mashed potatoes, green beans, and coleslaw. "You want this one?" he asked.

I tugged him by the collar and gave him a kiss. "I always want this one. But I'll take the plate as well."

His low chuckle, as always, made me wish for more privacy and less clothing.

* * *

WE ARRIVED at the gallery opening a little after seven, not late enough to be fashionable, but not so early that we had to wait in line. I'd been to a few art gallery shows in the city when I worked for Belliza. They were polite events, everyone quietly trying to impress everyone else with their knowledge of art history while nibbling on tiny, pretentious canapes that would starve a mouse.

Meadows and Fields Art Gallery show was not any of that. People gathered in groups, heartily eating Jane Beets marvelous chocolate creations. Except for the white chocolate doll figures, with black sugar pearls for eyes. Those were mostly untouched. We waved hello to a few people we knew, including Leila, Shawn, Reese, Jeanna Thompson, boutique store Monica, and the elder Mrs. Portman.

Even with her signature sweets making the rounds, I didn't see Jane at the event, and I was glad. Gilly was still angry with her, and I didn't want to break up a brawl on date night. I'd told Ezra what I'd seen in Jane's kitchen, and he'd talked to her this morning. She stuck to her story, and there wasn't enough evidence to arrest her at this point in the investigation. I wondered if The Diamond Shop burglary was a scheme to commit insurance fraud as well. Maybe, but that would be up to Ezra to find out. I wasn't interested in sniffing around gentle giant Dan Briggs and his souvenir shop.

Black partition walls were set up around the room to give it a maze-like quality that reminded me of Dolly's shop. The black surprised me because the vintage dolls were painted on black velvet, and it didn't offer a lot of contrast. I had expected the paintings to be weird. They not only met my expectations—they exceeded them. The porcelain dolls in the images were doing things like taking selfies on cell phones with the caption "Getting Dolled Up," doing video chats with the tops of the dresses on but no skirt or shoes from the waist down, captioned, "Dress Code Doll," but the one that made me cringe the most was the "Guys Swipe Right For Dolls" homage to dating apps.

"I feel icky being here," Gilly said.

Ezra, who was by my side, nodded. "It's definitely unsettling."

"They say good art evokes an emotional response," Tippi added.

"This must be some excellent art then." Pippa pressed her fingers to the base of her neck. "Because it's making me feel nauseated."

Marjorie held a wireless microphone and rang a clanging bell that sounded through speakers to every corner of the gallery. When everyone was silent, she said, "Friends and patrons, I welcome you here tonight to not only view Christopher Staten's Nesting Dolls open, but I hope that you will walk away tonight having had the experience of a lifetime."

Gilly leaned in close and whispered, "That's what she said. "

Ezra heard and stifled a laugh.

"Stop it," I whispered back. "You're going to get us

kicked out."

"Is that a possibility?" Gilly asked. "Because…"

I elbowed her, and she giggled.

"Tonight, you will see Nesting Dolls in a way that will explode all five of your senses." She pointed to the windows. "Davis, will you get the curtains?"

Davis, wearing all black, stood and yanked a cord that dropped black curtains over the two large windows that fronted the gallery, cutting off the sidewalk's view. Marjorie smiled. "Be prepared to have your senses rocked. You will touch, taste, see, hear, and smell the life that breathes from each one of these canvases."

Uh oh. "I don't like the sound of this," I said as the idea of doll-related trauma visions ran through my mind. "Maybe we should go."

Too late. The entire room pitched into the darkness. There was a murmur of surprise and nervous laughter throughout the gallery.

"And it begins…" Marjorie said ominously.

A loud sound was followed by the illumination of black lights. The velvet paintings morphed as paint that we hadn't noticed with the regular lights on, glowed, changing the appearance so that the dolls looked more modern in the dress and hairstyle, but also, some of the paintings became a more sinister commentary on the way people present themselves to the world and how they might appear in private.

"This is seriously spooky," Tippi said. "But kind of cool."

"I agree. I can see why Marjorie has been excited," I

said.

"It's over my head," Ezra commented. I heard Jordy laugh. Pippa's frosted pink lipstick glowed, but the rest of her was muted, and my chiffon top was practically see-through under the UV lights.

"Everyone, follow the arrows on the floor. Each destination will have written instructions. Mind your neighbor," she added. "We don't want any pushing or shoving."

Pippa was jittery next to me.

"Are you okay?"

"I need a bathroom, or I'm going to pee down my leg," she said. "It's urgent-urgent."

I'd been looking for an excuse not to smell the paintings, so I volunteered myself to help her find the restrooms. "You don't mind?" I asked Ezra.

"I can go with you if you want."

"That's okay." I smiled, doubtful he could see it. "You should enjoy the experience of a lifetime."

"How will you find me? Do you want me to wait somewhere?"

Ezra was wearing a dark blue shirt with a lightning bolt design across the front. The only thing I could see was his teeth from his grin and the lightning bolt. It was enough of a landmark to locate him in a crowd, though.

"I'll find you." I traced the bolt with my finger, raised up on my tiptoes, missed his lips, and planted a kiss on his chin. He grabbed me quickly and made the kiss right.

"I'm going to wet myself if we don't hurry," Pippa complained. "And I'm pretty sure urine shows up under this kind of light."

"That's true," Ezra said. "You should get going."

As luck had it, Marjorie had planned ahead with glowing signs that pointed to the exits and the bathrooms. We had to go behind another black curtain to get to the lit hallway with two bathrooms for men and women and a backdoor exit.

"I can see," Pippa said as her eyes adjusted to the new lighting. "And there's the bathroom." She pushed past me, her hand low on her stomach, and entered the door marked for women.

It was a relief to be out of the UV-lit gallery. I'd felt claustrophobic being squished between people I couldn't see. Even so, I hoped Marjorie had a lot of sales tonight. I felt the flush of a hot flash turn my skin into a wet dishrag. Ugh. Even my shirt was sticking to me. I couldn't understand why this was happening, but I hoped my OB/GYN had some ideas on stopping it.

Pippa was taking an extra-long time, so I went to the back door and tested it to see if it was unlocked so I could cool down. No such luck. I knocked on the men's room door. No answer, so I went inside. It was a single toilet, a urinal, a sink with soap, men's cologne, and a basket of neatly folded paper towels. I quickly grabbed some paper towels and wet them down.

I dabbed my neck and chest as I opened the door to the hallway. Davis Meadows was standing just around the corner. "I'm sorry," I said. "I just needed some water. I'll get out of your way."

A spray from the automatic air freshener in the men's room scented the air with pine.

Two men stand in the hallway. One has blond hair and is physically fit. I see the spade tattoo on his neck behind his ear. It's Grant. "I'm sorry, man. I don't mean to bug you at work. I just needed to talk."

"No problem," the other man says. "That's what I'm here for."

"I want to drink." The muted sound of Christmas music permeates the hall.

"Are you going to?"

Grant shakes his head. "I hope not."

"Do you want to tell me what's going on?"

"Carrie's mom has been making trouble for me for months. A few weeks ago, Carrie found out her real dad was a crook. The dude was serving life without parole for murder and some robberies. She's a hypocrite, man, and it just pisses me off."

"You can't control other people. You can only control yourself. You know that, right?"

"Thanks, Davis. I appreciate you talking to me."

The other man, who I now know is Davis, puts his hand on Grant's shoulder. "That's what sponsors are for."

I snapped out of the vision. Davis had a look on his face of a guy trying to make a decision. I'd just learned that he was Grant's sponsor, but I'd also learned he found out about Carrie's dad about the same time Dolly met her blackmailer.

Davis peered down at me. "What did Gilly mean yesterday when she said you guys were having a hypothetical debate as to whether you should turn someone in for a crime they've committed, even without proof?"

CHAPTER 23

"It was a philosophical debate." Loud classical jazz began to play in the gallery. I imagined it was the "hear" portion of the sense-fest.

Davis shifted his body to block my way out of the bathroom. "I hear things, Nora. Some things that are too incredible to be real, but one can't help but think…is it possible? Can Nora Black see the future?"

I let out a nervous laugh that ended with a derisive snort. "I'm not a seer. I can say with complete honesty, I do not see the future. If I could, I would have already picked the winning lottery numbers when the jackpot was up to nine hundred million."

He relaxed a little. "I thought it was nonsense."

"Complete and utter," I confirmed.

The space between Davis' body and my freedom was a sliver. I considered all the ways I could fit myself through and run. I hesitated to overreact. On the one hand, I was terrified. If Davis was behind the blackmail, the snake, and the murder, he was an incredibly creative psychopath. He would do anything not to get caught. Which meant I needed to get away and get away fast.

On the other hand, what if Pippa came out of the bathroom at the wrong time. Davis might hurt her if he thought she knew anything. She was eight months pregnant and in no shape to fight off a killer. And even if she wasn't, I couldn't leave my girl behind.

Davis moved his body closer, but I didn't step away because I knew if I allowed him to maneuver me out of the doorway, it would be easy enough for him to trap me. Of course, he could always shove me. I prayed he was still considering what I might or might not know.

The aroma of pine spray took me under once more.

"What am I supposed to do with this, Dolly?" I recognize Davis' voice now as he clutches a box of jewelry ranging from diamond and gold rings to platinum and gold necklaces.

Dolly pushes the box away. Her words are slurred, and her movements sluggish and imprecise. She's intoxicated. "Keep them, sell them, whatever. I don't care."

"How am I supposed to sell jewelry that was stolen?"

"Get a fence. That's the way we did it in the nineties."

He holds up a chunky gold ring that has channel-set diamonds all around it. "This is not what we agreed upon. I don't tell Carrie that you're a thief and a liar, and you give me cash."

"I don't have any cash left, Davis." She gives him the middle finger as she walks to the exit at the end of the hall. "That's all you're getting from me. If you push me, I will go to the police. I'll turn us both in. I might do it anyway. I don't

care anymore." She falls against the wall and presses her forehead to the door frame. "I just don't care. I'm losing everything."

"If you try and go to the cops, I swear I'll—"

"What? You're not going to do nuthin', you impotent mamma's boy." She turns toward him and waggles a finger at him. "You know how you kill a snake? You cut off its head. I learned that the hard way. And I'm going to cut your head off." She made snipping motions with her fingers. "Goodbye, Davis. I'll see you in hell."

"Not if I see you first."

"What's wrong with you?" Davis asked. "Do you have a seizure disorder?"

"Something like that." I tried to calm myself down, but fight or flight was real, and my body wanted to flee. "If you'll excuse me, I have to get back to the show."

"Nora!" I heard Pippa yell. "Nora!" she bellowed again. Damn it.

"Move, Davis," I demanded. "Get out of my way." I felt the sharp tip of a knife against my ribs.

"Let's take a walk out back," Davis said. "Me and you. No one else has to be involved."

"I'm not going anywhere with you."

"I just want to talk."

I swallowed the lump of fear in my throat. "People who want to talk don't bring knives."

His laugh chilled me. "You'd be surprised what a great conversation starter a sharp blade can be."

Pippa opened the bathroom door and waddled forward, holding her legs away from each other in a strange stance. "My water broke." She grabbed her stomach and groaned as she realized my predicament. "Oh, shiii-iiiiit!" she cried out.

Davis turned his attention away from me for the briefest of moments, and I brought my knee up hard and nailed him in his precious jewels. The knife pierced my skin but slid off my ribs as he double down, and I brought my head up hard under his chin. He staggered back. I charged the taller man with all my might, using my low center of gravity to knock him down.

Hitting a chin with your head hurts like hell, but it's useful in a pinch. I ignored my throbbing scalp as I directed Pippa. "Close the door and lock it. Don't come out until it's safe."

She moaned again as she did as I said. Damn it. That meant she was having another contraction. I wasn't a doctor, but it didn't take a medical professional to know that water breaking plus contractions meant this baby was coming. I worried if I left Davis behind with Pippa, he'd break down the door—or hell, he owned the place he probably had keys—and he would use Pippa to try and get away. Or punish me. A guy who would buy a snake to terrorize someone or take a meat tenderizer to their head was a guy who might do anything. I had to make him follow me.

His face was red, and his words blustery as he held up the knife. "You're dead now."

I squared my shoulders and told him with as much conviction as I could muster, "You'll have to catch me first."

I turned and ran up the hall and threw back the curtain as I entered the main gallery again. What I didn't count on was the fact that Davis, who was all in black, virtually disappeared as he entered the space. For the briefest of moments, I could see his teeth as he sneered at me, but then it was as if he had vanished.

On the other hand, I looked like a vibrant, neon jellyfish swimming through a dark ocean. The only other person who really stuck out was Marjorie, who had been painted up with glow-in-the-dark cosmetics, and she was bopping around with her microphone in hand.

"Lightning bolt, lightning bolt," I repeated. "Where is the ding dang lightning bolt?"

I couldn't find Ezra, and my panic was moving into seriously going to have a stroke territory. "Ezra! I shouted. "Jordy!" Gosh, anyone at this point would do.

Ari found me first. "Aunt Nora, are you okay?" She yelled. Even so, it was hard to hear her over the music. "What's on your side?"

I looked down. Where the knife had nicked me, sticky liquid coated my shirt, making the side look almost black. Blood, apparently, did not fluoresce.

I didn't have time to explain everything. I got close to her ear and yelled, "Pippa is in the bathroom," I said hurriedly. "She is having her baby. Find your mom. Find Jordy. Get your brother too. When you get Pippa, go out the back. Don't come back in here."

"You're scaring me," Ari said.

"I'm sorry. Look. You are the smartest girl I know. Now go be smart and do what I've said."

"If I find Ezra?"

"Tell him Davis Meadows is the guy. Tell him he has a knife."

An arm wrapped around my neck. "Don't tell him anything, little girl. Unless you want nice Aunt Nora to get her throat slit."

"Let her go," Ari said, her voice higher than I'd ever heard it.

"Why would I do that?" he asked.

We were a few feet from the small staging area where Marjorie danced. I hoped my eyeshadow was frosted enough to pick up the blacklight as I directed my gaze to Marjorie, who was holding a microphone.

"Go tell everyone," I said. "Go."

"Don't," Davis snarled, and like an idiot, he moved the knife away from my throat. I ran my booted foot down his shin and slammed my heel into his arch. He howled and brought the knife back, but I threw my head back and smashed his chin again. Davis was getting the full weight of my self-defense classes.

He let loose with a horde of colorful curses. Ari dashed to the stage, tackling poor Marjorie to the ground and grabbing her mic. There were a lot of shouts of surprise and outrage, but Ari was undeterred.

She must have found the on-off switch because I heard her say. "Hello, hello." Her words bounced over the music. "Mom!" she shouted. "Help. Aunt Nora is in trouble. Davis Meadows has a knife. Pippa is having her baby! Somebody, turn on the freaking lights!" The music made it impossible to know if help was coming or if anyone was listening.

"Get down from my stage, you maniac," Marjorie screeched. "You're ruining my show."

The guests were shoving each other left and right. They should have been running out the door, but instead, they were crowding the stage and cheering her on. Maybe they thought Ari was doing a performative piece because the more she said "Run," the more they cheered.

I made a break for the front light switches, maybe, just maybe. I could get there. If I could see Davis. I had a better fighting chance, considering right now I stuck out like a bright, neon thumb.

I pushed past several people, two of whom called me rude. What the hell? Maybe they thought Ari was part of the show because there was not nearly enough panic happening. I tripped over something on the floor, and it sent me sprawling forward, knocking over a stool. I reached out blindly, and my hands found purchase on a cloth that I hoped was the curtain.

It was not. I'd grabbed the tablecloth that rested under the chocolate fountain, and the sweet, warm liquid splashed over my head.

I slipped as I tried to get up. Davis was on me then, but he hadn't counted on the melted chocolate, making me hard to hold. I felt a sharp pain on my arm as he took a wild stab at me. I saw a lightning bolt, and my will to survive, which was already strong, kicked up a notch.

I reached out for something to fight back with. The metal stool was cool in my hand as I swung it as fast and hard as I could into his upper body. When he was off my legs, I kept swinging and kept swinging.

The lights came on, and the music went silent. Marjorie screamed. A few of the patrons seem to realize that actual danger had taken place and started rushing the door. Ezra, my lightning bolt guy, was dragging Davis, who had lost most of his struggle, away from me.

"Pippa," I rasped. "Baby."

My ex-husband Shawn was next to me now, his wife Leila on the other side pressing the yanked tablecloth to my wounded side.

"Here-eeeee!" Pippa squelched. Jordy was cradling Pippa in his arms and was carrying her toward the door. Tippi was right on their tail. "Nora!" she shouted.

I did the best I could to wave. "Go have a baby." My voice sounded like it had been filtered with tin.

"You're going to be all right," Leila assured me as she held pressure on my side.

"Christ, Nora," said Shawn. "You're a mess. Hold still. An ambulance is on the way."

"It's chocolate," I said. I licked my lips.

"There are two ambulances on the way," Reese said. "One for Nora and one Meadows." Her expression was incredulous. "You are one determined woman, Nora Black. How many of these jackasses do you have to beat in the head before they stop coming for you?"

Gilly squatted in front of me. "Hopefully, that was the last one." She wiped some of the chocolate sauce away from my face. "We don't bounce back like we used to, sis."

I gave her a thumbs up because words were hard. Besides, she wasn't going to get any disagreements from me.

Marco and Ari stood behind Gilly, and the look of terror on both of them was enough to make me want to weep.

"I'm okay," I told them. "Aunt Nora is fine." I shifted my gaze to Gilly. "Go to the hospital. Be with Pippa. She's going to need you."

"You need me, stupid."

"I'll be along soon enough." My head swam, and I felt woozy. I glanced over at Reese. "Where's Ezra?"

"He's getting the prisoner secured."

"He's here," I heard my guy say. "Thompson has Meadows." Ezra's face was transfixed with a mixture of rage and worry. Then his eyes softened as he moved Shawn out of the way and put his arms around me. "Everything's fine," he said. "I got you, sweetheart, and everything's fine now."

"Uh-huh," I agreed right before I puked all over his lightning bolt.

octor Scott Graham diagnosed me with multiple superficial lacerations, some hematomas, and a mild concussion.

I'd told him, "That'll teach me to use my head."

Dr. Scott had elevated his brows and smiled, revealing well-defined laugh lines. I could see why Gilly was attracted to him. He'd given me twenty-seven external sutures between my side and my arm, with another eight dissolving sutures in the side hole. Ezra had been by my side through the whole process, only leaving to check on Davis Meadows after the twins had arrived in my hospital room.

"That man tried to shish kabob me," I said as Ari set up her laptop so I could be with Pippa, even if only digitally for her birth.

"But you showed him." Ari came around the side of the bed and carefully hugged me.

"You're my hero, honey," I told her. "You saved my life."

"Vibe check, here. You straight-up saved yourself, Aunt Nora. I don't know what I would have done if anything bad happened to you."

"Nah, you can't get rid of me that easy."

Marco, who'd been quietly playing on his phone up until that point, said, "I think we can stop calling what happened to me at the game a fight. You demolished that creep tonight. And most of the chocolate."

"There are better ways to solve your problems than by lashing out," I said. The skin under his eye had turned yellow, and the swelling was almost gone. "Though, I agree that jerk on the court had it coming. Just don't tell your mom I said so."

"I can hear you," Gilly said through Ari's laptop. She was using her phone to connect the video chat in Pippa's room.

I gave Ari a look of reproof. "Give me a little warning next time," I said to the girl.

"From hero to zero," Marco teased.

I glanced from him to Ari. To her, I said, "You're my favorite." She grinned so wide it made my heart squeeze.

Marco rolled his eyes, but he was smiling.

Gilly turned the phone, so I could see Jordy holding Pippa's hand as she cradled a newborn swaddled in her arms. "Finally," I said. "I wish I was there. Give me all the details." We hadn't expected the new arrival so soon, but I was overjoyed to meet Baby Davenport-Hines for the very first time.

"It's a girl," Pippa told me. "Seven pounds. Two ounces." Her voice was tired but happy.

"Is seven pounds a lot?" I wrinkled my nose. "It sounds like an ungodly amount of kid to push through your vagina," I teased.

Jordy laughed. "She's perfectly healthy and extraordinary." He was beaming with pride.

"I think she looks like her Aunt Tippi," Tippi said, poking her head around.

"Wrinkled and bald?" I asked.

Gilly snorted in the background then took the phone closer to Pippa, Jordy, and their new bundle. "Isn't she exquisite?"

"Baby Davenport-Hines is stunning," I agreed. Her eyes were closed, and her tiny lips were puckered out. A slight noise escaped her. We all went gooey inside.

"She has a name," Pippa said.

"I voted for Tippi but lost," Tippi said.

"Hush." Pippa laughed gently, then blanched. "Ow. I'm still sore." She took her sister's hand. "I'm glad you're still here."

"If you don't mind," Tippi said. "I'd like to stick around for a while and watch my niece grow."

Pippa smiled. "I'd like that."

I loved watching our family grow, but there important business to discuss. "Don't just leave me in suspense. What's her name?"

"Judith Jean Hines," Pippa said with so much delight.

"How come Gilly's name is first?" I teased, unable to

keep the tears from falling. Pippa had given her daughter mine and Gilly's middle names.

"It sounded better in that order," Pippa said. "Do you approve?"

"Whole-heartedly. I wish I could be there." The doctor wouldn't let me leave observation, and the medical floor was no place to bring a barely hour-old baby. "Give J.J. a kiss from Aunt Nora and tell her I'll see her in the morning as soon as I'm given walking papers." Gilly zoomed in to Pippa. "You did good, momma," I told her. "I'm proud of you."

"Thank you, Nora." Pippa cleared her throat. Her eyes were watery with emotion. "Thank you."

Ezra returned shortly after we ended the video chat. He poked his head in the room and held up his hand. "How many fingers am I holding up?"

I rolled my eyes and grinned. "Is this going to become a thing?"

"The doctor said to watch for double vision." He was wearing a blue scrub top one of the nurses had given him since I'd ruined his shirt with a mix chocolate, vomit, and blood.

"Double you could be double the fun," I said.

Marco stood up. "I'm out," he said. He came over and kissed my cheek. "I'm glad you're okay."

"Me too."

"Take it easy, Easy," Marco said to Ezra.

"See you around," he replied.

Ari hovered at the door as if she couldn't decide whether to stay or go.

"What's up?" I asked her.

"I've been thinking about those online art auctions," she said. "It might be stupid, though."

"If it comes from you," I said, "that's not possible."

She opened her laptop again and pulled up the Artsy-Auction site. "Okay. Look at this piece. It's a blue heart painting with fourteen gold roses, and it's titled, Zero to Zero, blue heart of fire, one point three weight. The bid is currently at fifteen thousand dollars."

I nodded, not entirely following. However, in my defense, I did have a head injury. She pointed to a word. Fire had been spelled with a ph.

"Go on," Ezra said with interest. "What do you see that we don't?"

"Other than horrible art getting sold at outrageous prices," I added.

Ari nodded enthusiastically. "Exactly." She pulled up another screen. "This is where the leap in logic has to take place. I began to research stolen jewelry. In London, three months ago, a one-point-three carat sapphire necklace worth forty-five thousand dollars was stolen. It belonged to one of the royals and was on loan for a show. Now, Zero Two Zero is the national dialing code of London. So, we get London, Blue sapphire set in four-teen karat gold."

Ezra stared at Ari. "That's—"

"Stupid," she said.

"Brilliant," he corrected. "It's freaking brilliant."

"I love the way your brain works," I told her. "That's why Davis was so focused on those auctions. I bet if someone scoured his auction history, you'd find descriptions that match the jewels that David Summers and his crew stole. That son of a gun."

"So, this ArtsyAuction house is fencing stolen jewelry by selling it to the highest bidder. If I can get the Feds involved, will you explain this process to them? If we can link the jewels to Meadows, we can seal his fate."

Ari flushed. "Really? Yes. I want to help."

A WEEK LATER, we gathered together at Johnson and Billing's Funeral Home to say our final goodbye to Dolly Paris. She hadn't been a perfect person, but she'd been a friend, a peer, and for Carrie, a loving mother. After the memorial, followed by a graveside service, we all headed over to White Rose Church for a dinner that the church ladies had put together for Carrie. The way everyone had come together to support Carrie, including Grant, who hadn't left her side, I knew she—like I had—would form a family beyond the one she had been born with. One that was even stronger than blood because she chose it. It hadn't been forced on her through DNA.

Davis Meadows confessed to Dolly's murder. According to Ezra, it had become abundantly clear that the man was a narcissistic psychopath. His cleverness and his grandiose sense of himself had made him sloppy, especially when he was challenged. He'd been offered a reduced sentence of life with the possibility of parole in twenty years if he helped the FBI in their investigation into the online jewelry fencing scheme, but only if he made a complete confession to his other crimes.

And so, he admitted to buying the snake, but with the understanding that it had only been meant to frighten Dolly, not kill her. Even so, since the snake had bitten Carrie, that was one count of attempted premeditated murder since he'd known about Dolly's allergy. He'd admitted to killing Dolly, but only because she wouldn't tell him where she'd hid the cash. Again, he insisted it was her fault. Since he hadn't brought the weapon, he received a second charge of second-degree murder. He'd also stolen the dolls in her house, believing she'd hidden more money and jewels inside them. He was still confident that half a million in cash was still out there.

His mother, Marjorie, who I still believed was a good woman, was also his victim. She'd visited me in the hospital the next morning, horrified by what her son had done. I accepted her apology because it wasn't her fault that Davis was a psychopath. Even so, she would have to live with the stigma of his actions, and for that, I couldn't have been sorrier for her. At Carrie's request, she'd come to the funeral, but I'd noticed that she hadn't stayed for the meal.

As to Jane Beets, when pressed with the possibility of going to jail, she also made a full confession. She and Dan Briggs had both schemed to defraud their insurance companies, but just for enough to stay afloat. They thought if they kept the sum small, no one would look at it too closely. It turned out that the jewelry store smash and grab had been their inspiration.

Unfortunately for them, my nose knew the truth.

Because they confessed, the prosecuting attorney offered them a plea deal that included two years of probation, community service, and a hefty fine. I felt sorry for the two of them, but they could have ended up doing five years in prison, so they managed to escape the worst punishment. As for the jewelry store, it was still under investigation.

I sat at one of the cafeteria-style tables with Ezra, Gilly, Jordy, Pippa, Baby JJ, Tippi, and the twins. My family. I'd filled my plate with ham, funeral potatoes—a combination of potatoes, cheese, and sour cream baked in a casserole pan—,green beans with bacon and some kind of orange gelatin salad. If there was one thing church ladies knew how to do, it was throwing a heck of a potluck.

Ezra slid his hand over my thigh. "How are you feeling?"

"Okay," I said. "No headache today, so that's good." I was still bruised and a lot sore from the gallery brawl, but I was due to get my stitches removed in a couple of days, and after a few weeks, I'd be good as new. I needed someone to keep an eye on me at night, so I'd been staying at Ezra's place since my discharge from the hospital. We'd closed the shop while I was out since Pippa was on maternity leave. But Gilly had gone in one day for the electrician to fix the bell, and we added a few security cameras for good measure.

A hand on my shoulder drew my attention. Carrie

stood behind me. "Can I talk to you for a moment? Privately."

"Of course." I used Ezra for leverage as I eased myself up then followed Carrie down the hall to a room that was labeled *Church Secretary*.

She wore a necklace around her neck that had the gold band from her mom's treasure chest, along with the key. The silver and turquoise ring that had been taken from after the snake bite was back on her hand. It had been a promise ring from Grant. The feds had tied the emerald ring in the wall covey to an old burglary, so they kept it. They wouldn't release the fifteen grand to Carrie because it was with the stolen ring. They considered cash ill-gotten gains.

"I'm leaving town," she said. "When we get Mom's affairs in order, Grant and I will make a fresh start somewhere else…after a short road trip." She paused, giving extra weight to the words, *road trip*. "But I wanted to thank you for all you did for me. For what you did for my mom."

"I think she really loved your dad, and he never turned her in to protect the two of you."

Carrie nodded. "I know. Only David Summers wasn't my father. My mom left a letter with her lawyer when she'd made her will many years ago. She wanted me to know the truth, but as long as David was alive, he could ruin her life if he ever found out she'd lied to him. She'd joined the crew because of David Summers, but she'd stayed for Roger Tracy. The hair in the ribbon was Roger's."

"Roger Dodger." Cripes, the secrets that woman had almost taken to her grave. "Did she say anything else?"

Carrie smiled and touched the key on her neck. "She might have left a suggestion for places I might travel and things to find."

Like almost five hundred thousand dollars in cash? It would be considered ill-gotten goods, but the robberies happened before Carrie was born, and as far as I was concerned, this would be a case of finders keepers. Even so, I didn't ask because it was better for me not to know. Instead, I gave Carrie a brief hug, mostly because my ribs ached. "I hope your road trip is an adventure and that you find everything you're looking for."

I rejoined Ezra and our friends. He gave me a noisy kiss on the cheek. "Everything okay with Carrie?"

"She's good," I said. "Or at least, she will be."

As I sat there surrounded by the people who I loved and who loved me right back, I felt a piece of sadness for the loss of my mom and dad slip away.

Ezra cradled my hand in his, and he kissed my palm.

"I love you, Nora," he said, and I didn't doubt him one bit.

"I love you, too, Ezra."

I looked around at my friends, who were my family, and smiled. This aroma with a view smelled pretty darn sweet.

The End

PIT PERFECT MURDER

BARKSIDE OF THE MOON COZY MYSTERIES
BOOK 1

When cougar-shifter Lily Mason moves to Moonrise, Missouri, she wishes for only three things from the town and its human population. . . to find a job, to find a place to live, and to live as a human, not a therianthrope.

Lily gets more than she bargains for when a rescue pit bull named Smooshie rescues her from an oncoming car, and it's love at first sight. Thanks to Smooshie, Lily's first two wishes are granted by Parker Knowles, the owner of the Pit Bull Rescue center, who offers her a job at the shelter and the room over his garage for rent.

Lily's new life as an integrator is threatened when Smooshie finds Katherine Kapersky, the local church choir leader and head of the town council, dead in the field behind the rescue center. Unfortunately, there are more suspects than mourners for the elderly town leader. Can Lily keep her less-than-human status under wraps? Or will the killer, who has pulled off a nearly Pit Perfect murder, expose her to keep Lily and her dog from digging up the truth?

Chapter One

When I was eighteen years old, I came home from a sleepover and found my mom and dad with their throats cut, and their hearts ripped from their chests.

My little brother Danny was in a broom closet in the kitchen, his arms wrapped around his knees, and his face pale and ghostly. Until that day, I'd planned to go to college and study medicine after graduation, but instead, I ended up staying home and taking care of my seven-year-old brother.

Seventeen years later, my brother was murdered. At the time, Danny's death looked like it would go unsolved, much like my parents' had.

Without Haze Kinsey, my best friend since we were five, the killers would have gotten away with it. She was a special agent for the FBI for almost a decade, and when I called her about Danny's death, she dropped everything to come help me get him justice. The evil group of witches and Shifters responsible for the decimation of my family paid with their lives.

Yes. I said witches and Shifters. Did I forget to mention I'm a werecougar? Oh, and my friend Hazel is a witch. Recently, I discovered witches in my own family tree on my mother's side. Shifters, in general, only mated with Shifters, but witches were the exception. As a matter of fact, my friend Haze is mated to a bear Shifter.

I wouldn't have known about the witch in my genealogy, though, if a rogue witch coven hadn't done some funky hoodoo witchery to me. Apparently, the spell activated a latent talent that had been dormant in my hybrid genes.

My ancestor's magic acted like truth serum to anyone who came near her. No one could lie in her presence. Lucky me, my ability was a much lesser form of hers. People didn't have to tell me the truth, but whenever they were around me, they had the compulsion to overshare all sorts of private matters about themselves. This can get seriously uncomfortable for all parties involved. Like, the fact that I didn't need to know that Janet Strickland had been wearing the same pair of underwear for an entire week, or that Mike Dandridge had sexual fantasies about clowns.

My newfound talent made me unpopular and unwelcome in a town full of paranormal creatures who thrived on little deceptions. So, when Haze discovered the whereabouts of my dad's brother, a guy I hadn't known even existed, I sold all my belongings, let the bank have my parents' house, jumped in my truck, and headed south.

After two days and 700 miles of nonstop gray, snowy weather, I pulled my screeching green and yellow mini-truck into an auto repair shop called The Rusty Wrench. Much like my beloved pickup, I'd needed a new start, and moving to a small town occupied by humans seemed the best shot. I'd barely made it to Moonrise, Missouri before my truck began its death throes. The vehicle protested the last 127 miles by sputtering to a halt as I rolled her into the closest spot.

The shop was a small white-brick building with a one-car garage off to the right side. A black SUV and a white compact car occupied two of the six parking spots.

A sign on the office door said: *No Credit Cards. Cash Only. Some Local Checks Accepted (Except from Earl—You Know Why, Earl! You check-bouncing bastard).*

A man in stained coveralls, wiping a greasy tool with a rag, came out the side door of the garage. He had a full head of wavy gray hair, bushy eyebrows over light blue, almost colorless eyes, and a minimally lined face that made me wonder about his age. I got out of the truck to greet him.

"Can I help you, miss?" His voice was soft and raspy with a strong accent that was not quite Deep South.

"Yes, please." I adjusted my puffy winter coat. "The

heater stopped working first. Then the truck started jerking for the last fifty miles or so."

He scratched his stubbly chin. "You could have thrown a rod, sheared the distributor, or you have a bad ignition module. That's pretty common on these trucks."

I blinked at him. I could name every muscle in the human body and twelve different kinds of viruses, but I didn't know a spark plug from a radiator cap. "And that all means…"

"If you threw a rod, the engine is toast. You'll need a new vehicle."

"Crap." I grimaced. "What if it's the other thingies?"

The scruffy mechanic shrugged. "A sheared distributor is an easy fix, but I have to order in the part, which means it won't get fixed for a couple of days. Best-case scenario, it's the ignition module. I have a few on hand. Could get you going in a couple of hours, but…" he looked over my shoulder at the truck and shook his head, "…I wouldn't get your hopes up."

I must've looked really forlorn because the guy said, "It might not need any parts. Let me take a look at it first. You can grab a cup of coffee across the street at Langdon's One-Stop."

He pointed to the gas station across the road. It didn't look like much. The pale-blue paint on the front of the building looked in need of a new coat, and the weather-beaten sign with the store's name on it had seen better days. There was a car at the gas pumps and a couple more in the parking lot, but not enough to call it busy.

I'd had enough of one-stops, though, thank you. The

bathrooms had been horrible enough to make a wereraccoon yark, and it took a lot to make those garbage eaters sick. Besides, I wasn't just passing through Moonrise, Missouri.

"Have you ever heard of The Cat's Meow Café?" Saying the name out loud made me smile the way it had when Hazel had first said it to me. I'd followed my GPS into town, so I knew I wasn't too far away from the place.

"Just up the street about two blocks, take a right on Sterling Street. You can't miss it. I should have some news in about an hour or so, but take your time."

"Thank you, Mister…"

"Greer." He shoved the tool in his pocket. "Greer Knowles."

"I'm Lily Mason."

"Nice to meet ya," said Greer. "The place gets hoppin' around noon. That's when church lets out."

I looked at my phone. It was a little before noon now. "Good. I could go for something to eat. How are the burgers?"

"Best in town," he quipped.

I laughed. "Good enough."

Even in the sub-freezing temperature, my hands were sweating in my mittens. I wasn't sure what had me more nervous, leaving the town I grew up in for the first time in my life or meeting an uncle I'd never known existed.

I crossed a four-way intersection. One of the signs was missing, and I saw the four-by-four post had snapped off at its base. I hadn't noticed it on my way in.

Crap. Had I run a stop sign? I walked the two blocks to Sterling. The diner was just where Greer had said. A blue truck, a green mini-coup, and a sheriff's SUV were parked out front.

An alarm dinged as the glass door opened to The Cat's Meow. Inside, there was a row of six booths along the wall, four tables that seated four out in the open floor, and counter seating with about eight cushioned black stools. The interior décor was rustic country with orange tabby kitsch everywhere. A man in blue jeans and a button-down shirt with a string tie sat in the nearest booth. A female police officer sat at a counter chair sipping coffee and eating a cinnamon roll. Two elderly women, one with snowball-white hair, the other a dyed strawberry-blonde, sat in a back booth.

The white poof-headed lady said, "This egg is not over-medium."

"Well, call the mayor," said Redhead. "You're unhappy with your eggs. Again."

"See this?" She pointed at the offending egg. "Slime, right here. Egg snot. You want to eat it?"

"If it'll make you shut up about breakfast food, I'll eat it and lick the plate."

A man with copper-colored hair and a thick beard, tall and well-muscled, stepped out of the kitchen. He wore a white apron around his waist, and he had on a black T-shirt and blue jeans. He held a plate with a single fried egg shining in the middle.

The old woman with the snowy hair blushed, her thin skin pinking up as he crossed the room to their table.

"Here you go, Opal. Sorry 'bout the mix-up on your egg." He slid the plate in front of her. "This one is pure perfection." He grinned, his broad smile shining. "Just like you." He winked.

Opal giggled.

The redhead rolled her eyes. "You're as easy as the eggs."

"Oh, Pearl. You're just mad he didn't flirt with you."

As the women bickered over the definition of flirting, the cook glanced at me. He seemed startled to see me there. "You can sit anywhere," he said. "Just pick an open spot."

"I'm actually looking for someone," I told him.

"Who?"

"Daniel Mason." Saying his name gave me a hollow ache. My parents had named my brother Daniel, which told me my dad had loved his brother, even if he didn't speak about him.

The man's brows rose. "And why are you looking for him?"

I immediately knew he was a werecougar like me. The scent was the first clue, and his eyes glowing, just for a second, was another. "You're Daniel Mason, aren't you?"

He moved in closer to me and whispered barely audibly, but with my Shifter senses, I heard him loud and clear. "I go by Buzz these days."

"Who's your new friend, Buzz?" the policewoman asked. Now that she was looking up from her newspaper, I could see she was young.

He flashed a charming smile her way. "Never you mind, Nadine." He gestured to a waitress, a middle-aged woman with sandy-colored hair, wearing a black T-shirt and a blue jean skirt. "Top off her coffee, Freda. Get Nadine's mind on something other than me."

"That'll be a tough 'un, Buzz." Freda laughed. "I don't think Deputy Booth comes here for the cooking."

"More like the cook," the elderly lady with the light strawberry-blonde hair said. She and her friend cackled.

The policewoman's cheeks turned a shade of crimson that flattered her chestnut-brown hair and pale complexion. "Y'all mind your P's and Q's."

Buzz chuckled and shook his head. He turned his attention back to me. "Why is a pretty young thing like you interested in plain ol' me?"

I detected a slight apprehension in his voice.

"If you're Buzz Mason, I'm Lily Mason, and you're my uncle."

The man narrowed his dark-emerald gaze at me. "I think we'd better talk in private."

Want more? Got to www.
barksideofthemoonmysteries.com

PARANORMAL MYSTERIES &
ROMANCES

BY RENEE GEORGE

Nora Black Midlife Psychic Mysteries

www.norablackmysteries.com

Sense & Scent Ability (Book 1)

For Whom the Smell Tolls (Book 2)

War of the Noses (Book 3)

Aroma With A View (Book 4)

Peculiar Mysteries

www.peculiarmysteries.com

You've Got Tail (Book 1) FREE Download

My Furry Valentine (Book 2)

Thank You For Not Shifting (Book 3)

My Hairy Halloween (Book 4)

In the Midnight Howl (Book 5)

My Peculiar Road Trip (Magic & Mayhem) (Book 6)

Furred Lines (Book7)

My Wolfy Wedding (Book 8)

Who Let The Wolves Out? (Book 9)

My Thanksgiving Faux Paw (Book 10)

Witchin' Impossible Cozy Mysteries
www.witchinimpossible.com
Witchin' Impossible (Book 1) FREE Download
Rogue Coven (Book 2)
Familiar Protocol (Booke 3)
Mr & Mrs. Shift (Book 4)

Barkside of the Moon Mysteries
www.barksideofthemoonmysteries.com
Pit Perfect Murder (Book 1) FREE Download
Murder & The Money Pit (Book 2)
The Pit List Murders (Book 3)
Pit & Miss Murder (Book 4)
The Prune Pit Murder (Book 5)
Two Pits and A Little Murder (Book 6)

Madder Than Hell
www.madder-than-hell.com
Gone With The Minion (Book 1)
Devil On A Hot Tin Roof (Book 2)
A Street Car Named Demonic (Book 3)

Hex Drive
https://www.renee-george.com/hex-drive-series
Hex Me, Baby, One More Time (Book 1)
Oops, I Hexed It Again (Book 2)
I Want Your Hex (Book 3)
Hex Me With Your Best Shot (Book 4)

Midnight Shifters

www.midnightshifters.com
Midnight Shift (Book 1)
The Bear Witch Project (Book 2)
A Door to Midnight (Book 3)
A Shade of Midnight (Book 4)
Midnight Before Christmas (Book 5)

ABOUT THE AUTHOR

I am a USA Today Bestselling author who writes paranormal mysteries and romances because I love all things whodunit, Otherworldly, and weird. Also, I wish my pittie, the adorable Kona Princess Warrior, and my beagle, Josie the Incontinent Princess, could talk. Or at least be more like Scooby-Doo and help me unmask villains at the haunted house up the street.

When I'm not writing about mystery-solving werecougars or the adventures of a hapless psychic living among shapeshifters, I am preyed upon by stray kittens who end up living in my house because I can't say no to those sweet, furry faces. (Someone stop telling them where I live!)

I live in Mid-Missouri with my family and I spend my non-writing time doing really cool stuff...like watching TV and cleaning up dog poop

Follow Renee!
Bookbub
Renee's Rebel Readers FB Group
Newsletter